THE WILD BUNCH

THE WILD BUNCH

JAN GANGSEI

ALADDIN
NEW YORK LONDON TORONTO SYDNEY NEW DELHI

ALADDIN

An imprint of Simon & Schuster Children's Publishing Division

1230 Avenue of the Americas, New York, New York 10020

First Aladdin hardcover edition July 2017

Text copyright © 2017 by Working Partners Limited

Jacket illustration copyright © 2017 by Chris Danger

Also available in an Aladdin MAX paperback edition.

All rights reserved, including the right of reproduction in whole or in part in any form.

ALADDIN and related logo are registered trademarks of Simon & Schuster, Inc.

For information about special discounts for bulk purchases, please contact Simon & Schuster Special Sales at 1-866-506-1949 or business@simonandschuster.com.

The Simon & Schuster Speakers Bureau can bring authors to your live event. For more information or to book an event contact the Simon & Schuster Speakers Bureau at 1-866-248-3049 or visit our website at www.simonspeakers.com.

Jacket designed by Jessica Handelman

Interior designed by Mike Rosamilia

The text of this book was set in Adobe Caslon Pro.

Manufactured in the United States of America 0617 FFG

10 9 8 7 6 5 4 3 2 1

Library of Congress Cataloging-in-Publication Data

Names: Gangsei, Jan, author.

Title: The wild bunch / by Jan Gangsei.

Description: First Aladdin MAX edition. | New York : Aladdin MAX, 2017. |

Summary: On a weekend camping trip with their fathers, Hector, Jack, and Paul form an unlikely friendship as they brave the wilderness in search of the mythical Beast of Bear Falls.

Identifiers: LCCN 2016049812 (print) | LCCN 2017007812 (eBook) |

ISBN 9781481468299 (hardcover) | ISBN 9781481468282 (pbk) |

ISBN 9781481468305 (eBook)

Subjects: | CYAC: Camping—Fiction. | Fathers and sons—Fiction. | Adventure and adventurers—Fiction. | Imaginary creatures—Fiction. | Humorous stories. |

BISAC: JUVENILE FICTION / Action & Adventure / Survival Stories. | JUVENILE FICTION / Humorous Stories. | JUVENILE FICTION / Sports & Recreation / Camping & Outdoor Activities.

Classification: LCC PZ7.1.G357 Wil 2017 (print) | LCC PZ7.1.G357 (eBook) | DDC [Fic]—dc23

LC record available at https://lccn.loc.gov/2016049812

For Ted, Sven & Ava
My favorite Wild Bunch

AH, THE FIRST GLORIOUS DAY OF

summer break!

I'd managed to survive yet another year of brain-numbing homework, fill-in-the-circle-completely test forms, and whatever that stuff is that the cafeteria workers stick in Sloppy Joes.

Curled snugly in my nice warm bed, I was groggily considering all the things I'd do today: sleep till noon, shower in the lawn sprinkler, spend all afternoon lounging in the California sunshine . . .

HONK!

I bolted upright, whacking my head on the bunk

above me. My eyes watered, my legs twitched, and my heart tried desperately to eject itself from my rib cage.

Honk! Honk-it-y-honk-honk-honk!

This was definitely *not* on the list.

I fumbled in the darkness for the clock. . . . No, that *had* to be wrong. 6:47 a.m.

Huh? I held the glowing numbers closer to my face and blinked.

Six. Forty. Seven. *a.m.?*

HONKKKKK!

I dropped the clock. Was this some kind of joke?

"Luiz, my man!" I heard Dad from somewhere downstairs, followed by the front door slapping open and shut.

Who in the heck was Luiz? And why was my dad speaking in that ridiculous voice?

And then it all came flooding back. The truth I'd been trying to block out. The weekend *trip*.

Not Luiz . . . not already. He wasn't supposed to arrive until morning, and in my book 6:47 a.m. was *not* morning. It was definitely the tail end of the middle of the night.

I yanked the covers over my head. Next thing I heard was the sound of Dad's feet thundering up the stairs. *Urgh*. Did he always have to be so . . . enthusiastic? I peeked from beneath my blankets, eyes darting around the room in desperation.

One dresser. One second-story window. One bookshelf. And one truly pathetic-looking half-deflated beanbag chair.

Nowhere to run. Or hide. I flattened myself to the bed. Maybe if I kept real still, Dad wouldn't notice. . . .

I heard the door fly open. Whatever happened to privacy? Clearly I needed to invest in better security. A mantrap perhaps. Even a lock would do.

"Come on, sleepyhead!" Dad said with a clap.

I continued to play dead.

"I wonder where the little guy's got to," Dad said in the kind of silly voice usually reserved for six-year-olds. "I guess Paul musta packed his bags and left home for the summer. Oh well, I guess I'll have to go have fun without him."

Then, my covers were whipped off, leaving me clutching only my pillow. I opened one eye.

Dad stood there wearing a big goofy grin and an outfit ripped straight from the pages of a Wildlife Enthusiast catalog: khaki shorts, khaki vest covered with fishing lures, and coordinating khaki hat plastered with hooks, feathers, and fishing bobs.

He dropped the blankets, went to the window, then

whipped open the curtains. I screamed like a vampire exposed to light for the first time. Dad just laughed. The shiny metal pieces on his vest reflected the early morning sunlight in every direction, making him look like some sort of camouflage disco ball.

"Time to get up, Paulie! You haven't forgotten about Bear Falls, have you?"

"I tried," I mumbled. "Really, really hard."

"At least you're dressed," said Dad. "That's the spirit, buddy boy! As the Boy Scouts say, Always Be Prepared!"

That had nothing to do with the trip. I just couldn't be bothered to get undressed the night before, so I was still wearing my favorite long-sleeved Green Day T-shirt and nicely wrinkled cargo shorts. Wearing my clothes in bed also prevents Mom from getting near them. Because Mom irons *everything*: jeans, T-shirts, underwear, potted plants. Nothing's safe in the Adams house. Basically, the only way to avoid looking like Mark Twain Middle School's reigning King of Starch is to break my clothes in overnight. I mean, it's bad enough being twelve sometimes. The last thing I need is to be known as the twelve-year-old with the crease in his socks.

The clock hit 6:48. Dad just stood there, not taking the hint.

I sighed and sat up. I tried to smile, but it probably looked more like a grimace.

Dad winked. "Let's find your backpack, buddy." He went to my closet.

"Hey, don't go in—"

But he'd already opened the door. Hey, he couldn't say he wasn't warned. All my stuff—clothes (some clean, some not so much), sports gear, stacks of comics, old computer games, semiretired sneakers—came pouring out in an avalanche, burying him and swamping his cries. He came up like a drowning man, with an old jockstrap on his head. And somehow he was still grinning. He shook the stuff off and held out my backpack.

"Let's get cracking! Want to hit the road before traffic picks up!"

"Really? Do I have to, Dad?" I said. "I mean, I'm not much of a camper." I rubbed my crusty eyes again and coughed. "Or a morning person. How about I just stay here? I'll probably just drag you, uh, *outdoorsmen* down anyway."

Dad grinned and shook his head.

"I'll do extra chores for a month."

Another shake. The fishing lures clanked together.

"A year?"

Dad put his hands on his hips.

"The rest of my life!"

"Oh, come on, Paul. It'll be fun!" Dad said. "You wait and see!"

And this time, his smile faltered just a little, and he looked kind of desperate, so I stopped fighting. I knew Dad would never say it outright, but this trip meant a lot to him. He'd been working his butt off for the last year at school, taking on extra classes in the hope of a promotion to head of his department. Just a couple of days ago, they'd told him the job was going to someone else. All those late nights and weekends marking papers and preparing lessons had been for nothing. He pretended it didn't matter, but I knew my parents were worried about money—Mom had been laid off three months ago.

But "fun"? Let's just say Dad and I don't quite share the same definition of "fun." Like last summer, I wanted to go to the Super Mega Blast Water Park and ride the Cannon Shooter. Instead, Dad hauled me off to this tumbledown cabin in the middle of nowhere that was the childhood home of some Really Important Historical Figure who died three hundred years ago. Probably of boredom.

Don't get me wrong; it's not like I don't respect

the past and all. But with a history teacher for a dad, it kinda goes without saying I've seen enough Musty Old Places of Historical Significance to last an entire lifetime.

"Okay, chop-chop!" Dad said. He tossed the bag toward me and headed back into the hall, whistling "Yankee Doodle."

I plucked clothes from my dresser and floor and jammed them into my backpack, doing my best to squash any creases out of them. I was almost done when there was a knock on the door. "Hello, honey," Mom's voice said sweetly. "I have something special for you since you had to be up so early!"

Yes! Maybe this morning wasn't a total bust after all. I wondered if she'd made me pancakes. Or waffles. Or those little French toast things cut into triangles. I flung open the door expectantly and discovered . . .

Mom, standing there in her yellow bathrobe, holding a black T-shirt by the shoulders. "Father and Son Xtreme Adventures" was written across the front.

"Here!" she said. "I ironed this for you!" She pressed the still-warm garment to my chest. I crept back a step.

"Um, yeah, I don't think so," I said.

"Oh, come on," Mom said, raising it to put it over my head. "You'll look cute!"

Cute? Just what any self-respecting twelve-year-old wants to hear. "No, thanks," I said.

"I insist." Mom smiled. She held the T-shirt like it was a net and I was a wild creature about to be captured.

"But—"

"It'll make your dad happy."

I listened to the sound of my dad's whistling in the hallway.

"He sounds pretty happy already," I said.

"Paul," said Mom sternly. "This means a lot to him."

Ugh. Guilt trip coming. "I know," I said. "The job—"

"Not just that," said Mom, lowering her voice. "He feels bad because you guys never spend any time together."

"We watched a Giants game just last week!" I protested.

"*Quality* time," said Mom. "Sitting side by side shouting at the TV doesn't count."

She was right, I guess. There was a point when Dad and I did tons together—swimming, baseball, or just hanging out at the mall. When I was a couple of years younger, we even used to jam together in the garage while he taught me guitar. I'd lost interest, though. Between school, friends, and video games, I didn't have much time for Dad these days.

"Come on, Paul, do it for me," said Mom.

"Yeah, okay," I muttered, lifting my arms.

"Great! He'll be so happy!"

The world disappeared for a second as she put the T-shirt over my head.

Sadly, when it reappeared, nothing had changed.

I PEEKED OUT MY BEDROOM WINDOW.

A huge white SUV sat in front of the house, emitting sporadic honks like some sort of suffocating goose. Mrs. Delacourt across the street was glaring out her kitchen window in a hairnet.

Dad's voice boomed in my doorway. "Hey, buddy, I see you got your T-shirt on."

I turned and saw he'd changed into an identical one. "Snap," I said weakly. "You know, you and I could just chill out here at home, if you want?"

Dad laughed. "Just wait till you're in the great outdoors," he said. "It doesn't get any more 'chill' than that,

THE WILD BUNCH

as you kids say." He made a couple of air quotes with his fingers and winked. "Your friends Hector and Jack are really excited too."

"Right. Hector and Jack." I stifled a groan. "Just don't expect too much, Dad. They're not really my friends. They're *your* friends' kids."

He frowned. "You got along well at the Feinsteins' picnic last summer, remember?"

"Sure," I said. How could I forget? The picnic. First time I'd ever seen anyone swell up with hives after taking one bite of a hamburger. A hamburger! "Seriously, Dad. What sort of person is allergic to a burger?"

"Well, to be fair, Hector was only allergic to the sesame seeds in the bun," Dad said. "As far as I know, he doesn't have an issue with meat products. Just tree nuts. And gluten. And, um, dairy. Oh, and red dye number five. And . . ."

I turned so Dad couldn't see me roll my eyes. "Yeah, okay," I said. "And Jack, the guy who spent the whole party tossing stuff into the pool?"

"High-spirited, that's all. Full of energy," Dad said with a half chuckle. "Harmless."

"Sure," I said. "I think the Feinsteins' cat might disagree, though. It couldn't swim."

"Be nice, Paul," Dad said. "It's going to be fun!"

I rolled my eyes. That word again.

"Or *maybe*," said Dad, smiling, "you're too chicken?"

"What?"

He lowered his voice, hunched over, and threw out his arms like claws. "Maybe it's the Beast of Bear Falls you're scared of."

"Ugh! Not that again!" There was some story about a monster living in the park. It sounded like a cheesy horror film.

"Hector's father is bringing an old article he dug out," said Dad. "You wait and see. The Beast is real." He paused, looking over his shoulder. "Speaking of which."

I turned. "Ack!" I jolted backward.

My sixteen-year-old sister, Jeanie, stood at the door scowling, hair yanked tight in a ponytail and face caked in some horrible green goo. "Could you guys make any more noise?" she snarled.

"Gross," I said. "What happened to you? An alien barf on you while you slept?"

"Ha-ha." She perched her hands on her hips. "I'm exfoliating, moron."

"Ex-folly-what?"

"Ex . . . folllll . . . eeeee . . . ATE . . . ing," she said. "You know, removing the dead skin cells."

"Yeah? Better be careful . . . you might remove your whole head, then."

Jeanie scowled even more. The green stuff cracked a little. She looked like the Hulk's even grumpier daughter. I shuddered.

"Very funny," she said, narrowing her eyes at me. I turned around and grabbed my bag, hoping Jeanie would just crawl back into her cave. Instead, she burst out laughing.

"Well," she said, "at least I'm not wearing that lame-o T-shirt."

"Yeah, whatever," I said.

"I mean, 'The Wild Bunch'!" She clutched her stomach and doubled over laughing again. "Really fierce, Paul."

"What are you talking about?"

"The back of your shirt, burp breath."

"Now, kids . . . ," Dad said.

I yanked the shirt off and flipped it around. Across the back, block letters spelled out "The Wild Bunch." In bright orange. There was a feeble squiggle underneath that looked like it was trying to be a lightning bolt but gave up.

Dad shrugged. "Our club needed a name." He thumped my shoulder and headed out the door. "Hurry up, bud. Don't want to be late. Miss all the good fish, plus we need to pitch tents and . . . " He clomped down the stairs, still yammering about starting fires by banging rocks, and catching trout with his bare hands. Or maybe it was his teeth.

I dropped the hideous shirt on the floor. This had gone too far. I could get into the whole reconnecting-with-Dad thing. That was fine. But *this*? Dad had mentioned doing "a few things" together, but it had quickly spiraled into something else. Soon he was in touch with his old college buddies who had kids the same age; next there were conference calls. Apparently they'd visited Bear Falls themselves their freshman year and had a blast.

It was like I'd stumbled into some sort of midlife crisis mindscape and there was no way to wake up.

"There is no club," I muttered. "And even if there was, I'm not joining." I hoisted my backpack over my shoulders and shuffled after Dad into the hallway.

"See you later, Grizzly Man!" my sister yelled.

"Yeah, you'd better get back to the lab," I hollered back. "I heard Dr. Frankenstein was missing his latest experiment."

I trudged down the stairs. Dad was waiting by the front door, still grinning. We stepped into the bright morning sunlight. I squinted, took a deep breath—and something hit me with a thud on the back of the head.

"You forget something?" I turned to see Jeanie

standing at the base of the stairs, grinning maniacally, face mask shot to pieces. She pointed down at my feet.

I rolled my eyes and slapped my forehead, then grabbed the ridiculous T-shirt from the stoop and jammed it in my backpack. Dad was already climbing into the front seat of the SUV.

"C'mon, Paul!" he yelled. For good measure, Mr. Lopez honked three times.

I jogged halfheartedly to the car and cracked open the back door on the passenger side, only to be greeted by the wall that was Jack. He looked pretty much like I remembered from the last, and only, time I saw him: an oversize thug in a hockey jersey capped off with a mop of reddish-blond hair and a set of earphones. I stood there, tapping my foot, waiting for Jack to slide over. Instead, he popped off his right headphone.

"Not a chance," he said with a grunt. "I'm not sitting next to the puker." He jerked his head toward Hector, who sat on the opposite end of the bench seat. Hector smiled sheepishly, exposing a row of oversize teeth tangled in silver braces, and shrugged his bony shoulders.

"I get carsick sometimes," he said, swiping a clump of stringy black hair from his forehead.

"Oh, whatever." I climbed over Jack and sat down on

the little hump in the middle while Dad and Mr. Lopez fiddled with the car's navigation system.

"I think it's this button here," Dad said, jamming something with his finger. The car beeped.

"No, no," Mr. Lopez said. He poked another button and the sunroof above my head slid open. The next push popped the trunk. It's hard to believe sometimes that Mr. Lopez is actually some sort of computer genius. He's always got this perplexed look about him, like he's not quite sure where he left his own feet.

"So where's your dad, anyway?" I asked Jack. He lifted an earphone.

"He's got a game this afternoon," Jack said quietly. "He'll meet us later."

"A game?" I asked.

"Baseball," said Jack. He didn't offer any further explanation, so I didn't ask what team. Come to think of it, I couldn't remember his dad from the Feinsteins' either. But I'd done my best to wipe the whole event from memory, so that wasn't surprising. All I knew was that he was named Jack as well, which suggested a pretty poor imagination. I guessed it had to be a fairly important game for him to get out of the reunion with his college buddies.

Jack Junior snapped the earphone back on his head

and started playing a game on his cell phone. I turned my attention to Hector, who was picking a scab on his scrawny knee. He and I had actually attended the same kindergarten, but as far as I can remember, we weren't really friends then, either. His family moved across town later, so now we went to different schools.

"Hey, Hector," I said. He sat up, and I noticed he was actually *wearing* his Wild Bunch T-shirt, which was about six sizes too big and hung off him like a baggy dress.

"Hi, Paul." Hector nodded, then sniffled, sucked in a breath, and sneezed violently. Something green that looked disgustingly similar to the glop on Jeanie's face shot from his nose. I cringed and slid closer to Jack, who immediately elbowed me back toward Hector, without glancing up from his phone.

Hector sniffed, extracting a tissue from the backpack under his feet. A half-dozen bottles of allergy pills, creams, and inhalers tumbled out and rolled under the front seat. Hector scrambled to scoop them up while simultaneously stuffing the tissue high in his right nostril.

Up front, Dad and Mr. Lopez had apparently worked out how to start the navigation system, because a robotic voice suddenly announced, "Make a U-turn and proceed to the nearest intersection."

Mr. Lopez lurched the car into gear and pulled

forward, colliding with the curb. He jolted the car into reverse and backed up into a mailbox. A family of squirrels abandoned their nuts and fled in terror up the nearest tree.

"Sorry," Mr. Lopez said. "Rental. A bit wider turning radius than the Prius." He lurched the car forward again, muttering and pushing his thick glasses back into place. A fishing rod shot from the trunk and narrowly missed my head. I pushed it back with the rest of the camping gear: several more fishing poles, tents, sleeping bags, pillows, and one small blue cooler. I squinted in search of breakfast, lunch, or dinner.

"Hey, Dad," I said. "We packed food, right?" My stomach grumbled in emphasis. Jack actually looked up from his game and listened intently. There was no answer from the front.

"Dad?" I said. "Food? We packed stuff to eat, didn't we?"

"Uh, sure, Paul," Dad said. "We packed *rugged* food." He gave a knowing nod to Mr. Lopez, who reached over to fist-bump him. And missed.

I looked to see if there was an ejector button that could shoot me out through the sunroof.

Let's just say I've pretty much had my fill of Dad's so-called rugged food. Every time Mom goes out of town to visit Great-Aunt Beatrice, Dad and I survive on a diet of beef jerky, Spanish peanuts, and canned sardines. It's about the only time I'd rather be at the Great Oaks food court with Jeanie. I hated to think what he was planning for this trip.

After a few more bumps and lurches, we made it onto the road. Mr. Lopez nailed the gas and we shot down Cherrydale Drive toward the highway at the supersonic speed of, oh, two miles an hour. Excellent. At this rate, we'd arrive at Bear Falls just in time for the end of summer break.

Dad rolled down his window and took a deep breath. "Ah yes," he said. "Fresh air . . . the great outdoors . . . this is going to be an awesome weekend! Isn't it, boys?"

Mr. Lopez glanced in the rearview mirror at us.

I shrugged. Hector sneezed. Jack belched and blew it out of the side of his mouth in my direction.

A whole weekend stuck in the wilderness with the missing link and the one kid on the planet allergic to the outdoors. Lucky me.

I closed my eyes and leaned back on the seat. "Somebody pinch me," I said under my breath.

"Ek-thuse me?" Hector said, stuffing a tissue in his left nostril and breathing through his mouth.

"Noth—," I started to say, when a meaty hand to

my right reached over and squeezed the skin on my forearm. Hard.

"Ow!" I said. "What was that for?"

"You said 'pinch me.' " Jack grinned, and for the first time I noticed there was a big black gap where his left front tooth should have been. I wondered if the thing had been knocked out by a hockey puck, lost in a fight, or if Jack had just yanked it loose for kicks. I rubbed my arm.

Whatever. Jack just confirmed what I'd suspected all along. This wasn't a nightmare—it was really happening. If I slept long enough, perhaps I'd wake up when it was all over.

I DID ACTUALLY MANAGE TO SLEEP, thankfully, and woke up when Jack shoved me two hours later. My neck ached like I had whiplash, but there was little chance of that with Mr. Lopez driving. We'd obviously merged onto the highway, but something seemed to be wrong with the car because everyone was shooting past us and several drivers were giving us angry stares. Then I realized the cruise control was set to 50 mph—well below the speed limit. I checked the navigation system: only three million miles or so until we reached the park. At the moment our ETA was three p.m., without breaks.

I slumped my shoulders and rested my chin on my chest. Up front, Dad and Mr. Lopez began discussing the best sort of bricks to use as patio pavers and where to invest their savings for maximum return. My eyelids drooped again.

"Yep," Mr. Lopez said. "My broker says the smart money is in pig futures these days."

"Pig futures," Dad said. "Interesting. Well, you know what they always say: Ride the bull, beat the bear. Or maybe it's ride the *hog*." Dad let out a weird piglike snort. Mr. Lopez laughed so hard he accidentally pressed the accelerator. The car lurched forward, my head whipped back, and my eyes shot open. I rubbed my neck.

Jack elbowed me. "Stay on your side," he said.

"What side?" I said. "I don't even have a side!"

"Good one, Bill!" Mr. Lopez said, and attempted a high five. But Dad was leaning over, rooting through a bag by his feet. Mr. Lopez's hand swung through the air.

Dad sat up grinning, holding a CD case. "You brought it!" he said.

Mr. Lopez grinned back and wiggled his eyebrows.

"Brought what?" I asked, actually beginning to feel somewhat hopeful. If there was anything that could speed up the journey, it was music.

Dad responded by loading the CD and hitting play.

The twang of banjos and screech of fiddles blasted through the speakers. Soon after, a harmonica broke in, accompanied by high-pitched shrieking that could only have resulted from a person being accidentally electrocuted. Dad and Mr. Lopez slapped their knees and sang along.

"I'm so lonesommmmme, I could cry! Got my fingerrrrrrs in my eyes!"

I slapped my own hands over my ears.

"What is this?" I said, cringing.

"It's the Cornhuskin' Catfish Callers, or Triple C as they're known," Dad shouted over the dueling banjos. "Back in college, we used to play this nonstop."

"Yep," Mr. Lopez said. "Best bluegrass-country–smooth jazz fusion band ever. I have all their albums!"

"You mean these people got a record deal?" I asked.

"Twenty-seven albums and counting!" Mr. Lopez exclaimed. "And I brought them all. Should last the whole trip!"

I sank down in my seat. There was no way I'd ever get any rest on this drive.

Dad and Mr. Lopez went back to singing.

"I've got the cornhuskin' blues, from my hat down to my shoes!"

"Anyone else feel the sudden urge to square-dance?"

I muttered. "Or maybe just throw yourself from the moving vehicle?"

Jack, with his headphones on, seemed oblivious.

"I don't dance," Hector said matter-of-factly. "Ver-
tigo. And jumping from the car at our current rate of
speed would be highly dangerous and would likely result
in death."

"You don't say," I answered. "Thanks for that."

Jack stuffed a handful of candy in his mouth, licked
his fingers, and belched. "You're welcome," he said, without taking his eyes off his phone. I glanced in his direction. A half-dozen candy wrappers were littered around
his feet. My stomach grumbled.

"You got any extra?" I asked, pointing at an empty
Twizzler package. Jack just sneered. "Guess not," I said.
Deciding to find out what Dad meant by "rugged food," I
leaned over the seat into the cargo area, flipped the top on
the little blue cooler, and found myself face-to-wriggling-
face with . . .

A container of squirming night crawlers stuck in ice.

"Ugh," I said, holding back a retch and slapping the
lid shut. "What are those disgusting things for?"

Mr. Lopez's eyes peeked in the rearview mirror.

"Bait!" he said.

"What are we trying to catch, the plague?" I said.

"Historically, the plague has been transmitted via rat," Hector said. "Actually, via fleas on rats. So you don't need to worry. You can't catch the plague from a bunch of worms."

"What a relief." I sank back into my seat. A car loaded with teenagers in bathing suits cruised up next to us, windows down and bass thumping. Surfboards were strapped to the roof. A girl wearing oversize sunglasses and a Billy's Beach Club T-shirt poked her head out, the wind lifting her sun-streaked hair.

My eyes opened wide. I leaned over Hector, who was staring at the seatback in front of him, and rolled the window down.

The guy driving the car leaned out his window and yelled, "Surf's up, little dudes!" The car then sped forward and switched lanes. I craned my neck and watched it disappear, surfboards wobbling on the roof rack, and elbowed Hector.

"Oh man," I said. "Did you see that?"

"See what?" Hector said, staring straight ahead and sniffling. "I can't turn to the side. Makes me feel queasy."

"Seriously?" I said.

"Seriously," he said. "What was it?"

"Nothing," I said. "Just people going somewhere fun."

"Hey now," Dad said. "Camping is fun! You just wait and see!" He and Mr. Lopez began singing again.

"Give me that crawfish, sing me a diddy, we're headed down to Catfish City!"

"Actually," Hector said, still focused on the seatback like it contained the answers to life's greatest riddles, "camping can be quite hazardous. For example, there was the terrible hiking incident of 1996 in which two campers fell to their deaths in a giant crevasse. Not to mention the cougar attack of 1971 that resulted in a camper losing two limbs and an eye. Then there was the blinding hailstorm of 2011. . . ."

I stared at Hector as he continued rattling off morbid camping facts. Hikers bitten by snakes. Snakes eaten by foxes. Foxes gobbled up by wolves. The universe collapsing on itself.

"And of course," he said, "let's not forget the Donner party."

"The *Donner party*?" I said. "But they weren't even camping. They were traveling cross-country in a wagon and were trapped by snow in the mountains. It's summer. And we're just going to Bear Falls!"

Hector shrugged. "The point is, it pays to be prepared. Which is why I brought this." Without turning his head, Hector yanked a beat-up old book from the seat pocket and handed it to me. I read the cover: *Survival in the Wild*. The pages were worn and dog-eared, and

Hector had highlighted several passages and stuck Post-it notes on others.

I slapped the thing shut and stuck it back into the seat pocket. "Thanks," I said. "I didn't think I could get any more excited about this trip."

"You're welcome," Hector said, completely without irony.

I turned in Jack's direction, but he just shoved a handful of M&Ms in his mouth and grunted, "Nope."

I figured things really couldn't get any worse. But then we rounded a curve and the car suddenly slowed. Horns began to honk. I looked out the front window: red brake lights as far as I could see. Mr. Lopez tapped the steering wheel.

"Hmm," he said. "Appears to be a bit of a traffic jam."

"Maybe we should just turn around and go home," I offered.

"Nah," Dad said. "I've got a better idea. We'll have a sing-along! Did them all the time when I was a kid on family vacations. Always made the ride go faster."

He flicked off the CD player and started to sing.

"Ninety-nine bottles of Coke on the wall, ninety-nine bottles of Coke!"

He paused and glanced back. "C'mon, you boys know how it goes!"

I groaned and joined in. *"Take one down, pass it around, ninety-eight bottles of Coke on the wall."*

Hector sneezed and rubbed his nose. "Can't drink anything carbonated."

"But you're not drinking it," I said. "You're just singing about it."

Hector shrugged. "Doesn't matter."

"Ninety-eight bottles of Coke on the wall . . . take one down, pass it around . . ."

I started to think my head might explode. By the time we'd cleared the wall of bottles, we had progressed all of twenty feet.

"I'm not sure that made anything faster," I said. "In fact, it might have caused time to move backwards."

Jack popped off his earphones and brushed the piles of candy wrappers from his lap. "Actually," he said, "it made me thirsty. Can we stop for a drink?"

Mr. Lopez shook his head. "Afraid not," he said. "Got to make up for lost time. Want to reach the park before nightfall. You can have some of this, though." He scrabbled between the front seats and pulled out a sweaty thermos, handing it back.

Jack grabbed the thermos in both hands, unscrewed the cap, and guzzled down an enormous gulp. His face immediately turned a strange shade of green.

"Ugh!" he said, quickly pulling the container from his lips and gagging. "What is this stuff?"

"Protein shake," Mr. Lopez answered proudly. "Made it myself."

"What's in it?" Jack said, nose pinched.

"Well, got a few strawberries, bananas, raw eggs . . ."

"Raw eggs?" Jack swallowed hard and began to suck in shallow breaths.

"And wheat grass and dandelion puree," Mr. Lopez continued. "From my own backyard, even!"

Jack puffed his cheeks out, hand over his mouth.

"I think he gets the picture," I said, pressing as far away from Jack as my seat belt would allow.

"And of course," Mr. Lopez said, "my secret ingredient . . . ground anchovies with a touch of fresh-from-the-garden coriander! Gotta get my omega-3s!"

Jack's hand flew from his lips and he promptly spewed out a lovely green concoction flecked with half-chewed M&Ms and bits of Twizzlers. It spattered all over seat in front of him and ricocheted onto my shirt.

"Ugh!" the rest of us screamed. I covered my mouth to keep from hurling too. Mr. Lopez quickly lowered the windows. Dad tossed a pack of wet wipes over the seat.

"You know," he said. "It's always wise to check what

you're about to eat *before* you put it in your mouth."

Jack groaned and clutched his stomach. I pulled out a wet wipe and dabbed it on my shirt, trying not to breathe.

"Yeah," I said. "I bet you're glad you didn't sit next to pukey Hector, now, aren't you?"

MR. LOPEZ EASED OUR ROLLING

stinkmobile off the highway to a rest stop. The moment he shifted into park, we leapt from the car. I sucked in huge gulps of fresh air, wiping M&M flecks and who-knows-what-else from my arms.

"Ack," I said. "How many bags of candy did you eat, anyway?"

Jack trudged off toward the bathroom without answering. Hector and I followed.

"Don't feel bad," Hector said in the direction of Jack's lumbering frame. "I once threw up on the teacup ride at Disneyland. And let me tell you, it doesn't get much worse than *spinning* puke. You wouldn't believe how far that stuff can fly! Took, like, a half hour to get it all out of my sister's hair!"

I put my hand over my mouth. "Seriously? Are you trying to kill me?" I said from behind my palm.

Hector just raised an eyebrow and shrugged. "What's the big deal?" he said. "Vomiting is merely the body's natural response to outside stresses such as extreme motion, viral infection, excessive eating, or exposure to . . ."

I tuned Hector out and went into the bathroom. It smelled like a lemon-Lysoled version of the pukey car. Jack was already holed up in a stall, producing the most fantastic-sounding explosions I've ever heard come from a person.

I headed straight for the sink, washed my hands and arms, and hurried back toward the door before the methane could render me unconscious. But before I could grab the handle, Hector yelled out my name. He must have followed me inside.

"Paul, stop!" he said.

I froze, hand in midair, and glanced over my shoulder. "What?" I said.

He rushed at me, a paper towel clutched in his hand. "You don't want to touch that," he said.

"Huh?"

"The doorknob," he answered. "More germs on one of those things than inside the toilet bowl, you know." He grabbed the handle with his paper towel and twisted it open.

"Uh, thanks," I answered, stepping outside. Dad and Mr. Lopez were already back in the car, loudly singing with the windows rolled down.

For a moment, I considered going back into the bathroom and licking the doorknob. Maybe if I contracted something awful, Dad would be forced to take me home. A few days lying in bed playing my DS while Mom brought me warm soup didn't sound half bad. . . .

Honk! Honk-it-y-honk-honk!

Dad poked his head out the window. "Hurry up, boys!" he said as Jack and Hector appeared behind me. "Got to keep on schedule!"

I reluctantly climbed back into the car, wedged once again between my two non-BFFs, and we rolled back into the bumper-to-bumper traffic. Straight ahead, a huge billboard advertised: GREAT ADVENTURE AMUSEMENT PARK, 10 MILES.

"You know," I offered, pointing at the sign, "maybe we should go there instead. It's a lot closer."

Hector peered between the seats and squinted. "An

amusement park?" he said with a small gulp. "Are there teacups?"

"We're not going to any amusement parks," Dad said. "We're going on a *real* adventure!" He clicked his fingers in the air. "Luiz, you bring that article we talked about?"

"Sure did!" Mr. Lopez said. He reached under his seat, digging around for something, and the car jerked quickly to the right and back to the left. "Check this out," he said, producing a beat-up old magazine.

I took the faded yellow *National Geographic* and set it on my lap. The cover featured a weird, grainy picture of a bunch of tall pine trees with something in the middle that had been smudged away by a huge coffee stain. I read the heading. *"The Beast of Bear Falls,"* I said. *"Missing link or myth?"*

Jack, who had been turned away with his face pressed against the window, suddenly spun around. "The what?" he said with a grunt. Yeah, I should've known the words "missing link" would get his attention.

"I don't know," I said. "Let me check it out."

I could hear a slight tremble in my voice. I'd thought the article would be printed from some weird website for people who'd been abducted by aliens or thought Elvis was still alive. Not a *real* published piece in a *legit* magazine bought by millions of people. I flipped through the pages to the dog-eared article and read out loud.

"One early summer's day, explorer Mo Harper ventured into the woods at Bear Falls State Park armed with a backpack, tent, and camera, intent on proving the existence of the mythical 'Beast.' He never came out again."

I stopped short, eyes wide. Hector made a strange squeaking noise. Jack elbowed me. "Keep reading, dude," he said. "This is getting interesting!"

There was an inset picture of Mo Harper—long curly hair, goofy grin, open-necked shirt, with a camera hanging on a strap. He looked like a nice guy. Maybe only twenty-five or so.

I cleared my throat. *"After an exhaustive search, the only sign of young Mr. Harper was a battered camera, recovered in the forest near the waterfalls. And the only clues about Mr. Harper's fate were these pictures, discovered when the film was later developed by the sheriff's department. . . ."*

I flipped to the next page, which featured a series of photographs framed in black boxes. The first was the fuzzy picture from the front cover—only instead of a coffee stain, there in the lower branches of the tree sat a large, hair-covered Sasquatch-like man-beast. A few more pictures of the waterfall, trees, and a rocky crevice followed.

The last picture was a close-up of a giant paw-like appendage coming toward the camera lens.

Hector pulled out his inhaler. After several large puffs he leaned back.

I could see Dad looking at me. "You're quiet all of a sudden," he said.

I closed the magazine, checked the date. "This was thirty years ago," I said.

"Yes," said Hector. "It's highly unlikely that creature—if it even exists—is still alive."

"Really," said Mr. Lopez. "You're an expert on cryptozoology, are you?"

I couldn't see his face, but I could tell he was smiling. They were making fun of us.

"That thing comes near me," said Jack, "it's gonna get a serious smackdown." He did some sort of punch combination on the back of my dad's headrest.

"Easy!" said Mr. Lopez. "This is a rental car!"

I was looking again at the cover. The photo was so crappy, but it somehow seemed more convincing because of that. Something about the blurring and poor exposure gave me the chills.

"What if we found it?" said Dad, eyes shining gleefully.

"All of the evidence would suggest," Hector said,

pointing at the magazine, "that we'd be better off *not* finding the Beast."

"Oh, don't be such a baby," Jack said. "It would be awesome. In fact, I'm gonna find that thing, trap it, and make a fortune! And you losers can come visit me in my mansion." He popped his earphones back on.

Up front, Dad and Mr. Lopez shifted their conversation back to the thrilling topic of patio bricks (horizontal or vertical, the existential question!). I attempted once again to nap. This time, I fell into a deeper sleep, dreaming of waterfalls and woods and giant man-beasts. . . .

The next few hours passed slower than the movement of tectonic plates. We stopped a few more times for the bathroom and food. Jack ate his own body weight in candy, and we listened to the complete seventies oeuvre of Triple C, along with commentary from Dad on their musical progression and experimentation with punk-folk fusion.

I was jolted awake when the car suddenly lurched around a corner, knocking me right onto Jack's lap. He shoved me away with a grunt. I sat up, rubbing my eyes. The clock said 4:45 p.m.

"We're here, boys!" Dad announced gleefully as the car rolled to a stop in front of a gate. A small wooden guard booth covered in faded brown shingles sat to our left with a green-and-yellow BEAR FALLS STATE PARK sign nailed to the side. Tall pine trees framed the road.

The guard booth door swung open, and a woman wearing a crisp green button-up shirt, green shorts, and a no-nonsense expression stepped outside. Mr. Lopez rolled down the window. The woman leaned in, sunlight catching the faint black-and-gray mustache above her lip.

"Looks like we tracked down the Beast already," muttered Jack.

"Good evening," she said. "Welcome to Bear Falls State Park."

"Thank you," Mr. Lopez said. "We've already done our registration." He handed her a form and a wad of cash. The woman handed him a map in return.

"Campsite number twenty-four," she said, standing up straight and pointing. "Go 'bout three miles, turn left at the pine trees, and then follow the signs."

"Thanks," Mr. Lopez said. He began to roll up the window. The woman's hand landed on top of it.

"Just be careful," she said, bunching her thick eyebrows together. "Got a fog rolling in this evening. Makes it mighty hard to see the forest for the trees around here!" She snort-laughed at her own joke.

"Okay then, thanks again," Mr. Lopez said. The gate lifted.

"Hey, wait a minute," said Jack. The lady turned. I thought he was going to say something rude, but he ruffled through the candy wrappers and other detritus for the *National Geographic*.

"You ever see this Beast?" he asked.

I expected the guard to say something funny, but she looked deadly serious. "You guys just be careful, okay? Cell service is spotty up there. If you get into any trouble, just find a road and head downhill."

She went back to her hut, and Mr. Lopez pulled away through the gate.

"That wasn't a no," said Hector.

"I guess she likes to mess with people's heads," said Dad. But even he looked a little bit nervous.

The trail road was narrow, winding between the tall trees. Through the open window, I could hear the distant rush of water. The air was heavier here than back at home—damp and sticky. As we made our way deeper into the park, a thick mist descended on the road like a giant cloud. Mr. Lopez began to drive even slower, going from, oh, five miles an hour to quite possibly negative two. He squinted into the fog.

"Can't make out any signs," he said. "Can barely see the road. This may take a while. . . ."

Jack began to squirm uneasily.

Hector took a bunch of shallow breaths. "All this fog is making me queasy," he said. "You sure we haven't missed a turn?"

Just then a foul odor filled the car, like a dozen rotten eggs left in the hot sun for ten days.

"Oh man!" Jack covered his nose. "Who farted? My lungs are melting." He looked around all of us, then settled his glare on me. "It was you, wasn't it?"

"Me?" I said, gasping for air. "Don't they always say, the one who smelt it dealt it? Besides, I heard you in that bathroom. Sounded like cannon fire."

"Then you know I don't do the silent-but-deadly," Jack retorted.

Hector stayed suspiciously quiet, gaze focused straight ahead.

"You know, I distinctly remember a very similar, ahem, stink bomb in our dorm room freshman year, Luiz," Dad said.

"Is that so, Bill?" Luiz said. "If I remember correctly, you were busy trying to impress one Christine King with your guitar playing and were more than happy to pin that one on *me*."

"Huh," Dad said with a smirk. "Well, I wasn't the one who'd just eaten a plate of beans, and she did marry me, so . . ."

Mr. Lopez glanced over at Dad and gave him a friendly shove. "Then you ought to know I have a gut of steel," Mr. Lopez said, rubbing his belly. "I'm immune to the power of the bean. . . ."

Hector sat up straight, arms crossed in front of him like he was trying to ward off a vampire. "DAAAAAAAAAAD!" he yelled.

"Huh, what?" Mr. Lopez said.

"Look out!" Hector screeched.

We all turned our attention back to the road, just in time to see a herd of deer run from the edge of the forest—and leap directly in front of the car.

"AAAAAAAAGH!"

Mr. Lopez jammed on the brakes and jerked to the right. I closed my eyes, mouth frozen in a terrified O, and braced for impact.

THE CAR SKIDDED SIDEWAYS, SCREECH-ing loudly as the undercarriage scraped across the gravel shoulder. With a loud thump, and two popping sounds, we came to a sudden stop.

I slowly opened my eyes . . . to see the front air bags deployed. As they deflated, Mr. Lopez stayed frozen, with a stiff-armed grip on the steering wheel. Dad sat next to him, feet pushed against an imaginary brake in the footwell. Jack had his hands on his head, and Hector was hyperventilating into his shirt.

The herd of deer bounded away—uninjured—and disappeared into the forest.

"Whew, that was close," Mr. Lopez said, uncurling his white knuckles from the steering wheel and wiping his forehead. He gently tapped the accelerator. The wheels spun uselessly. "But . . . it appears we are stuck," he said.

"Maybe we could push it out?" Dad offered. "We've got some strong guys back there."

The car gave a grinding sound, then dropped another foot, leaning slightly in the ditch.

"I'm not a mechanic, but that sounded lethal," I said.

Jack shoved me. "This is all your fault!"

"My fault?" I said. "Maybe we wouldn't be in this ditch if you hadn't farted. Next time, do us all the courtesy of holding it in!"

"Like I said, it wasn't me," Jack said. He shoved a thick finger in front of my face, pointing at Hector. "It was probably him. He looks like the sneaky type."

Hector's cheeks flamed red. "Unlike other people in this car, I'm not a Neanderthal. I roll down a window if I have to break wind."

"Who are you calling a Neanderthal, nerd?" Jack said, leaning over me. A huge whiff of beef jerky, Cheetos, and candy breath hit me right in the face. I pinched my nose shut.

"Well, if the unibrow fits . . . ," Hector started.

"Okay, okay, boys," Mr. Lopez broke in. "I think we

can all agree that the deer are at fault." He pulled out his cell phone. "Let me just call the rental company. . . ." He dialed a number and began to yap. "Uh-huh. Yep. Uh-huh. Really? That long? Okay, I see." He clicked off the phone and sighed.

"What is it, Dad?" Hector said.

"Afraid they can't get out to us until tomorrow," Mr. Lopez answered. "We're a bit too . . . remote to reach tonight."

"Oh, great," Jack groaned. "We're gonna be stuck here all night in this tiny car?" He wiggled his shoulders back and forth, banging me with every other movement, then stopped and sniffed the air. "Ugh!" he said. "And someone farted *again*?"

Jack threw open the door and leapt from the car. The rest of us followed, fingers pointing, accusations flying. I could barely hear a coherent word over all the shouting—until Dad stuck his fingers in his mouth and let out a loud whistle. Everyone fell silent and turned to look at Dad. He held his palms in the air.

"Hey now," he said, smiling. "This isn't how the Wild Bunch face adversity! We're not going to have our fun ruined by a fart . . ." He glanced back at the car. One of the wheels was crooked and flat. "Or a lack of viable transportation! Nope!"

Dad whipped the park map from his pocket, tapped his finger against the paper, and smiled even wider. "By my calculations, we're just one mile from the campsite. We can take a shortcut trail from the road to get there. So everyone, grab some gear and let's go!" He shoved the map back into his pocket and flung open the trunk.

Okay, now would probably be a good time to point out once again that my dad is a *history* teacher. Not geography. Or math, even. *History.* And if past experience is any indicator of future performance, I should have realized right then that following a confirmed optimist with a poor sense of direction deep into the woods might not be the best of plans.

Still, off we went, carrying backpacks and bedrolls, sleeping bags and tent bags. We headed up the road until we reached a gravel forest track between the trees. In the distance, the ground rose to endless forest-clad mountains.

"How big is this place?" I asked.

"About forty thousand acres," said Mr. Lopez, breathing heavily. "Plenty of places for a yeti to hide."

"Doubtful. The yeti is a Himalayan myth," said Hector helpfully.

"Maybe it's on vacation too," said my dad, chuckling to himself.

We trooped single file down the narrow trail, my

backpack heavier every step of the way, the sun dipping lower and lower. I lost track of time a bit, and the trees grew denser and more overgrown the farther we got. Every time Jack took a step, I had to dodge the fishing poles slung haphazardly over his shoulder. Jack weaved and a hook swung side to side, narrowly missing my nose.

"Hey!" I said. "Watch it."

"Watch what?" Jack answered through a mouth full of candy.

"Ugh," I said, ducking. "If you're going to assault me the entire way, the least you can do is share your candy."

Jack glanced back mid-chew and rolled his eyes. "Oh, all right," he said. He dug around in his pocket and extended his hand. I looked down at his red-, blue-, and yellow-streaked palm covered in little brown pieces of chocolate that I assumed had once been M&Ms.

"That's disgusting," I said.

Jack shrugged. "You want 'em or not?"

"We'll get a fire going when we reach the campsite and cook some food," said Dad. He checked the map again. "Should be there any minute now."

My stomach grumbled. "Oh, what the heck," I said, scooping the M&Ms up and shoving them in my mouth. Not half bad. I spat out a piece of lint and kept chewing. Hector sneezed behind me.

"I'm out of tissues," he said. I turned around, just in time to see him drag his drippy nose across his forearm.

"Not far, I think," Dad said from up front. He turned the map sideways, then upside down, which wasn't encouraging. We slowed by a fork in the road, where a dirt path ran off slightly downhill to the right. He pointed along it. "Should be just a few more clicks in this direction!" He began marching again.

"Wait, what?" Hector said. "What's a few?"

Dad had on this really awkward forced smile, just like the time he put Jeanie's homecoming dress in the washing machine and shrank it two sizes. "Like I said, not far now!" he answered.

"So will your dad be able to find us?" Hector asked Jack.

"Of course," he replied. "He's not dumb. Plus, he can actually drive in a straight line, unlike your dad."

"Hey, he was only asking," I said.

Jack grumbled something.

"What team does he play for, anyway?" I asked.

"Huh?" said Jack.

"You said he was playing baseball."

"You wouldn't have heard of them," said Jack. He put on a burst of speed to catch up with my dad and Hector's.

We slogged on, maybe another mile so, until finally

we heard the sound of gently lapping water. A clearing appeared in the distance. Just beyond, I could see a large lake with a half-dozen empty campsites marked with little wooden signs in front of it.

"Told you I'd get us here," said Dad.

We made it to number twenty-four and flung our gear on the ground. As far as I could tell, we were the only campers out here, and that worried me. To be fair, the place was pretty amazing: still, crystal-clear water, trees as far as you could see, mountains. It looked like a postcard.

Hector fell on top of his bag. He looked pale and sweaty.

"No time to lie around," said Dad, checking his watch. "We need to get our tents pitched before night falls."

Hector pulled himself to his feet. We unpacked the tents. Jack unfurled his first, and I swear it covered most of the campsite.

"I think that's bigger than my house," I said.

"All the latest technology," Jack said. "Built-in lanterns, super moisture-wicking material, the best engineering available." He tipped over a vinyl bag and about a hundred poles and stakes clattered to the ground. Jack stared at them, mouth twisted to the side.

"And you need a degree in engineering to put that thing together?" I said.

"I'll figure it out," Jack said, holding up a spike and glancing back and forth between it and the huge expanse of material at his feet.

"Good luck," I muttered.

"Hey, Paul!" Dad shouted, waving both hands over his head and smiling, as always. "Help me set up our accommodations!"

I trudged over. Dad picked up a small bag, pulled open the drawstring, and dumped out our tent. It smelled like a closet in a nursing home—all mothballs and stewed vegetables and disinfectant. Dad unfurled the thing onto a tiny patch of earth. It was about as big as a coffin.

"Are we supposed to sleep on top of each other?" I said.

"Ha-ha!" Dad clapped my back. "Good one. Now grab a pole and let's put this baby together."

I did what Dad said and jammed a tall pole into the ground. Dad shook the tent over it. The canvas hung limply around it.

"Hmmm," Dad said, rubbing his chin. "That doesn't look quite right."

"You have the instructions?" I asked. The tent was so old that any "instructions" were probably written on parchment.

"Instructions?" Dad said with a laugh. "We don't

need instructions! Just put these stakes around here." He pointed to the edges of the tent.

"Whatever you say, Dad." I pounded the stakes into the ground, securing the corners of the tent. When I was done, it tilted strangely to the left. I shook my head.

"I still don't think that looks right," I said.

"Nonsense," Dad said. "It looks perfect!" He climbed inside and lay down, his calves and feet sticking out the end.

There was a strange ripping sound behind me. I turned to see Mr. Lopez standing with a pole in his hand. Hector stood next to him, holding a piece of torn fabric.

"Oh my," Mr. Lopez said. "And I thought all natural fibers were supposed to be strong. . . ."

"Ha!" Jack said. We glanced across the campsite to where Jack stood in front of his mini-mansion, arms folded smugly across his chest. "See it and weep!" He held up a small remote control, pushed a button, and the whole thing lit up like a Christmas tree.

"Whoa," Hector said.

"Eh, it's just a tent, son," Mr. Lopez said.

"A very nice, very luxurious, not-at-all-ripped tent," said Hector.

Mr. Lopez took out a roll of duct tape. "We'll have ours fixed up in no time."

Mr. Optimist, aka my dad, clapped his hands together. "So, now that we're all set up, who's hungry?"

"Me," Jack said. He grimaced and slapped his arms. "But first, who has the bug spray? I'm getting eaten alive!"

"Right," Dad said, rooting through his bag. "Mosquitoes descend in the evening. Can get pretty bad out here in the woods. But don't worry, got some repellent right here. . . ." Dad's brow furrowed. "That's strange, I could've sworn. . . ." He shook the bag upside down. A few pairs of underpants and a can of Mom's French Lady body spray rolled out.

"Oops," he said, cheeks red. "Guess I grabbed the wrong bottle."

A swarm of mosquitoes buzzed around my head. I swatted hopelessly at them. Instead of going away, they seemed to multiply. "Ugh, what are we supposed to do, then?"

"I know," Hector said. "We packed some sunflower oil for cooking. We can use that. It's a natural repellent."

"Good thinking, son," Mr. Lopez said.

"Only problem is, we need to mix it with an essential oil to make it work," Hector continued.

I held up Mom's French Lady perfume. "How about this? *Parlez-vous français?*"

"Hey, I don't want to smell like a mom!" Jack protested, nose scrunched.

"Wouldn't work anyway," Hector said. "Too many artificial chemicals."

"Ooh!" Mr. Lopez said. "I've got it!" He scrabbled through his bag and pulled out a first aid kit. "Cod liver oil!"

"Brilliant," Hector said. He set to mixing the two oils together in an empty water bottle, then passed the bottle around. Jack took one whiff and gagged.

"Gross," he said. "I don't want to smell like a fish."

The rest of us smeared the stinky concoction over our skin. By the time we were done, we smelled like the inside of a bait shop.

But on the plus side, at least the bugs—and Jack—were staying far away.

"OKAY, LET'S GET A FIRE STARTED,"

Dad said. "Why don't you boys gather up some wood?"

"You mean you didn't bring any of those pretreated logs?" Jack asked.

"Don't be ridiculous," Dad replied. "What would be the fun in that? Besides, we're surrounded by trees! Hurry along. Luiz and I will organize the supplies."

Jack, Hector, and I trudged into the woods on a narrow forest track. Actually, Hector and I trudged. Jack swung from the tree branches, grunting like a gorilla. So much for finding a Beast; we'd brought our own.

After a few yards, Hector slowed and knelt on the

path. He picked something up with a pair of tweezers and held it in front of his face.

"What are you doing?" I said. "We're supposed to be gathering firewood, not pebbles."

"Actually," Hector replied, dropping the pellet into a plastic bag and standing, "this is rabbit dung."

Jack leapt down from a tree branch and landed with a thud on the path. A cloud of dust puffed around him.

"Hold on," he said. "You're scooping up poop?"

"Technically," Hector answered, "it's animal excrement and it is part of the research for my Science Stars program. I'm bagging and identifying as many types of feces as possible." He gave his hands a generous squirt of antibacterial gel.

Jack threw a glance at me, as if to say, *Is this guy for real?*

"Finding a wide variety of animal dung is not as easy as you think," Hector continued.

"Yeah, significantly easier for you than finding a girlfriend," Jack said.

"Come on, guys," I said. "The sooner we can gather some wood, the sooner we can go back to the campsite, go to sleep, and get this trip over with, okay?"

I stepped off the path, heading toward a pile of fallen tree branches. I'd been camping and hiking before a few times, but this place was really something else. As soon as I was away from the trail, it felt different. Kind of scary, actually. It was a real wilderness—not like the local parks I'd been to. Looking straight up among the soaring trees, I saw patches of blue sky through the branches. It was so peaceful, it was hard to believe we had the whole place to ourselves. You could scream and shout out here, and no one but Mother Nature would hear.

Then something whacked me in the face. Something stringy and sticky.

"Blech." I backed up, peeling long strands from my hair, lips, and eyelashes. I walked right into Jack.

"What's your problem?" he shouted.

I was spitting and brushing my arms. "Just walked into a spider's web."

Hector inspected me clinically, blinking behind his thick glasses.

"Well," he said. "I guess that explains *that*." He pointed at my shoulder. I glanced down to find a shiny black spider the size of a bicycle crawling across my sleeve.

"Ack!" I screeched a little too loudly and flicked it off. I took a step backward, shuddering. Jack ran over, laughing, and scooped the spider off the ground. He wiggled his hand, letting the disgusting creature crawl up and down across his fingers. There are only two things in this world that freak me out (besides being wedged in a car forever between Jack and Hector): spiders and snakes.

"Don't be a wimp," Jack said. "It's just a little bug."

"Actually," Hector said, "it's not a bug. 'Bug' is a scientific term, meaning belonging to the Hemiptera order, and that taxonomical classification doesn't include spiders."

"Whatever," Jack said. "Maybe I'll name him Jack the Third. He's so cool. I mean, look at that red mark on his back. It's like a giant blood spot!"

Hector's eyebrows shot up and he took a few steps back.

"What?" I asked.

He quickly pulled the guidebook from his pocket and thumbed it open, glancing back and forth between the page and Jack's hand.

"*Black bulbous body, red hourglass shape on the abdomen . . . ,*" Hector read out loud. Jack talked over him.

"You and that stupid book," he said. "Blah, blah, blah, spider . . . blah, blah, blah, poop . . ."

Hector slapped the guidebook shut. "Uh-oh, that's not just any spider. It's a black widow!"

Jack stopped talking. "A black . . . *what* did you say?"

"A black widow!" Hector said urgently. "One of the most dangerous spiders known to man!"

Jack let out a high-pitched shriek that sounded an awful lot like my sister the time she discovered her Instagram account had been disabled. He shook his hand and the spider fell, dangling from his fingers by a single strand of silk. "Get! It! Off! Me!" he shouted, jumping up and down.

Hector swatted the thread with his guidebook, knocking the spider loose. It scurried off into the underbrush. He smirked.

"Guess it's not such a stupid book after all, is it, Junior?" he said.

WE SCOOPED UP AS MANY SPIDER-
free sticks and branches as we could carry and headed back to camp. Jack swung a giant branch in front of his face like a baseball bat, narrating an imaginary game the entire time.

"Aaaaand it's the bottom of the ninth," he said in a fake announcer's voice. "Seven to seven. The bases are loaded. Two outs. And Jack Gracie Senior is up to bat. That crowd is on their feet. . . ."

"Yo, Jack," I said. "What team does your dad play for again?"

He ignored me and kept talking. "Strike one . . . strike

two . . . and *craaaaaack!* It's going . . . going . . . it's gone! Home run! The crowd goes wild!"

Jack swung his stick, whacking it against the tree branches overhead, and we came through the clearing to our campsite. Dad waved in front of the lopsided tents.

"Right here, boys," he said, pointing toward a small hole in the ground. We dropped our wood into the pit. Dad immediately picked up two dry sticks and grinned at Mr. Lopez. "How about we start this baby the old-fashioned way?"

Mr. Lopez smiled back and nodded. Dad began rubbing the sticks together. After about a minute, all he'd managed to do was peel away some dry bark. His forehead was covered in a sheen of sweat. He paused and held the twigs in front of his nose. "Huh," he said. "Looks a lot easier on *Survivor.*"

"Let me give it a try," Mr. Lopez said. He took the sticks and flipped them around, as though a fuse might be located at the other end. While he rubbed the sticks pointlessly together, Dad picked a camping shovel off the ground.

"Hey, boys," he said. "While we get the fire started, why don't you go dig us a latrine?"

"A what?" Jack asked.

"Latrine," Dad said. "For depositing human waste."

Jack looked around the campsite. "Funny. Where are the toilets?"

Dad laughed. "Did cave people need toilets?" he said, and handed Jack the shovel. "Make sure to dig the pit at least two feet deep and a hundred feet from the lake's edge."

Jack stared at the shovel in his hand like it was actually made from human waste.

"Hurry along, boys," Dad said. "It'll be too dark to see what you're doing soon."

Jack dragged the shovel across the ground, muttering to himself. Hector and I followed.

"Oh," Mr. Lopez said. "Forgot to mention. Your dad texted, Jack. He won't get here until tomorrow afternoon at the earliest. That deal he's working on is getting ready to close. Sorry, buddy."

Hector and I glanced at each other, eyebrows raised. As we walked away from the dads, I called after Jack, "I thought he was at a baseball game."

Jack blushed. "He is."

"So what's this about a deal?" Hector asked.

"He was taking some clients to the game," said Jack, still not meeting anyone's eye. "Like a hospitality thing."

He stomped ahead, shoulders sagging. I would have

said something else, but Jack really didn't look like he was in the mood.

We reached a small clearing in the trees. Jack stopped, brushed away some fallen leaves, and started to dig hard, like he really hated that little patch of earth. I was actually feeling a little bit sorry for him, until he flung a clump of soil at me and Hector.

"No way am I pooping in a hole in the ground," he said.

"Better than in your pants," I said. Hector snorted. Jack paused, shovel in midair, and glared at us. For one brief, satisfying moment, I pictured him tumbling head-first into a full latrine and sinking up to his neck. He pushed the shovel into Hector's hands.

"Your turn, Pooper Scooper," he said.

Hector could barely lift the shovel, and it was painful watching him try to dig, so I took over. When I'd fin-ished, we had a small trench about a yard long, a foot wide, and a foot deep. I even left a neat pile of earth to shovel in afterward. Can't say the thought of squatting over the thing filled me with excitement. I stuck a branch in the ground to mark it, and we headed silently back to camp. Dad was standing in front of the unlit campfire, holding a stick in one hand and using the other to strum it like a guitar.

"Give me FI-EYE-ER!" he sang in a falsetto voice, hips swiveling, eyes closed. Have I mentioned Dad is also in a band? Well, he is. Not a stick-playing band, of course. He plays guitar for this classic rock group that practices every Sunday. They're called Young at Heart, and they sometimes even play at our annual neighborhood barbecue.

I cleared my throat. Dad opened one eye, then the other. "Heh," he said. "Didn't hear you boys coming. Not having much luck with the fire, I'm afraid. . . ." He let out an embarrassed chuckle.

"Might be time for Plan B," Mr. Lopez said. He reached in his bag, pulled out a pack of matches, and held them in the air.

"Well, I suppose . . . ," said Dad. "I mean, I coulda done it the old-fashioned way."

With a quick flick of the wrist, Mr. Lopez ignited the birch bark under the twigs and sticks. Soon the campfire was roaring, sending a plume of smoke into the deepening sky. I looked at everyone's faces in the firelight and saw smiles all round. This was kinda cool.

We assembled a few large logs around the flames and sat on them, letting the fire warm our hands and faces. Dad shook his canvas sack upside down. A cast-iron pan, a pack of hot dogs, and a couple of cans of baked beans rattled onto the ground.

"Dinner!" he announced, picking up a can of beans. He stretched an open palm toward Mr. Lopez. "Can opener me."

Mr. Lopez peered into his own bag, rooting around a bit, then a bit more. I just knew what was coming. "Uhh . . . seems we have a bit of a problem. It said on the spreadsheet that Jack Senior was bringing the can opener, remember?"

"Oh," Dad said. "That is a bit of a problem." He tried banging the can against a log and managed to put a small dent in the top. Mr. Lopez took the can and inspected it.

"Perhaps if we calculate the velocity needed to cause structural damage . . ." He banged it too.

"Hold on," I said. "Let me try." I flipped the can over, then found a flattish rock and stood the can on top.

"I can't wait to see this," said Jack, smirking.

I began to rub the can back and forth as fast as I could. After a minute my arm was aching and I was working up a sweat. I turned the can over to check. The metal was scuffed and worn.

"Still no genie?" said Jack. "We're going to starve before you ever get it open."

He snatched the other can, flicked open his pocket-knife, and began to attack the rim like a psycho with a thing for murdering cans. I continued with my rubbing.

After another minute I heard Jack crow, "I'm in!" Then a moment later, a snap. "Oh."

Jack's knife was broken off in the can's top. Then my own top began to feel loose, and some bean juice spilled out. I turned the can over and saw the lid had come off.

The sweet and pungent smell of baked beans wafted through the air. Everyone but Jack cheered. "Nice work, son!" said Dad.

We managed to open up the other can enough to pour out the contents into a pan, and Hector stirred the pan over the fire. I don't think lukewarm hot dogs and beans have ever tasted so good. Jack licked his plate and let out a huge burp.

"Excuse me, excuse me, from the bottom of my heart," he said. "If it came out the other end, it would have been a—"

"Yeah, we know what it would have been," I said.

"So what's for dessert?" Jack leaned over and dug through the rest of our supplies like a stray dog pawing through trash. "You can't be serious." He took out a couple of cans of Spam. "I didn't know they still made this stuff."

"Not sure they do," said Hector's dad, grinning. "I found that in the back of the garage."

"How old is it?" asked Hector.

His dad shrugged. "No idea. I don't think it goes bad, though. It's meant to survive a nuclear Armageddon."

Jack triumphantly held up a bag of marshmallows. "Dibs!" He pulled the plastic apart and a bunch of giant marshmallows flew through the air and scattered around his feet, rolling in the dirt. I grabbed the bag from his hands and nodded toward the ground.

"Those are all yours," I said.

I passed the bag around, and we all jammed a few gooey marshmallows on sticks and held them over the fire. I carefully twirled mine to achieve the perfect golden crust. You have to do it just right or you'll be left with still-hard marshmallow in the middle. Or even worse, a charred outer shell. Okay, it might not be five-star cuisine, but marshmallow roasting is an *art*.

Unless, of course, you happen to be Jack. I watched from the corner of my eye as he jammed six marshmallows onto his stick and thrust it directly into the flames. In a matter of moments, the whole thing was on fire. Jack yanked it back out and jumped up and down, puffing and blowing, spittle flying everywhere.

"Okay now," Mr. Lopez said, leaning to the side to avoid the spray and grimacing. "Food is for eating, not playing with, young man."

Jack just laughed and flung the smoldering

marshmallow over his head into the darkness. "Do-over!" he said, grabbing a new one.

"This is great," Dad said. "You know, all that's missing is some music!"

"No, it's really not," I said.

But he went over to our tent and came back with his guitar anyway. He began to sing.

"We're going on a bear hunt.

I'm not afraid!

What's that?

Tall trees!"

He paused. "Come on, Paul! You used to love this book. I bet ya remember the words too. Join in!" He ran his fingers over the strings.

"Can't go over them,

Can't go under them,

Got to go around them!"

I shoved another gooey marshmallow in my mouth. Normally, such behavior would have made me want to curl into a ball, but I'd reached peak shame some time ago. And I remembered what Mom had said about what this trip meant to Dad. No one else was singing, just him. So I started too, quiet at first, but getting louder.

"We're going on a bear hunt.

I'm not afraid!

What's that?

Ooh, it's mud!"

Hector wrinkled his nose and grimaced. "Eww," he said.

"It's just a song," I told him. He shook his head.

"No," he answered. "That *smell*. What's that horrible smell?"

"I dunno," Jack said, licking gobs of marshmallow off his stick. "Maybe the dung in your pocket, Pooper Scooper?"

"Nope." Hector sniffed the air. "That is most definitely not excrement. It's . . ."

"Something burning!" I shouted. "And it's not the fire!"

Dad dropped his guitar. I dropped my stick. And we all jumped to our feet and spun around, just in time to see Jack's massive tent ignite in a burst of flames.

"NOOOOOOOO!" JACK YELLED, running toward his tent, arms over his head like his own pants had caught fire. He came to an abrupt stop, shielding himself from the heat. Funny what a rogue marshmallow can do.

"Hurry," Dad said. "Grab anything you can find to hold water. We've got to put it out before we start a forest fire!"

We gathered pots, pans, the cooler, and even a couple of hats, and raced to the lake—scooping up water, running back, and dumping it on the fire. I'm not sure if it was us, or just the fire burning itself out, but none of the trees caught fire. Jack's tent, however, had been reduced to a pile of smoldering ashes with one singed metal pole poking straight up in the middle. The stench of burning synthetic material made me want to gag.

"I can't believe this," Jack said. "That tent was brand new! Top of the line! All the latest features!" One of the built-in lanterns popped and fizzled out, sending another twist of smoke into the sky.

"But evidently not fireproof," said Hector.

Jack shot him a look that could have frozen lava.

Dad clapped Jack on the shoulder. "Don't you worry," he said. "We still have two perfectly functional tents."

I glanced at the Lopezes' tent with the giant hole covered by duct tape, and ours lilting sideways next to it. I guess "functional" is sort of like beauty. All in the eye of the beholder.

"Here's what we'll do," Dad said. "You boys can have our tent. Luiz and I will take the other one. Let's all get some rest. It's been a long day."

Dad and Mr. Lopez headed off to set up their sleeping bags.

"Aww, man," Jack moaned as soon as they were out of earshot. "I'm not sleeping next to Pooper Scooper."

"What makes you think I want to sleep next to you, Junior?" Hector retorted.

Jack gritted his teeth. "You'd better sleep with one eye open," he said.

Hector snarled back and held up his hands, raising one foot like the dude in that old Karate Kid movie—the one my dad always feels compelled to quote every time we wash his car. *Wax on, wax off. Wax on, wax off!* Hector wobbled. Jack reached his pointer finger out, ready to push him over.

"Okay, enough," I said, stepping between them. "Just take it easy. I'll sleep in the middle. I'm getting kind of used to being stuck between you two."

We unfurled our sleeping bags and shimmied inside the tent, settling shoulder to shoulder. There was barely room to stretch out, let alone roll over. Jack thrashed around and scratched himself.

"I can't get comfortable," he said. "It smells like fish oil in here."

"Funny," Hector said. "I really can't smell anything over the aroma of burned tent."

Jack grunted and extended an arm across my face toward Hector. I shoved it away.

"Seriously, just relax," I said, channeling my best Dad voice. "Tomorrow is a new day. Maybe we can go to the falls."

"Or hunt the Beast," said Jack.

"There's no Beast," said Hector.

"You wish," said Jack. "Hey, maybe we'll find that dude's remains. Harper, wasn't it?"

"If the Beast left anything," I added, warming to the conversation.

Hector was wriggling farther down into his sleeping bag.

It was quiet for a little while, but I couldn't sleep. "Anyone know any ghost stories?" I asked.

Hector groaned.

"Sure!" said Jack. "You want 'The Headless Hitcher'? Or 'The Puppet Master's Surprise'?"

Something howled in the distance outside the tent. Hector yanked his sleeping bag right up to his nose, and even I jumped a bit.

"I think Pooper Scooper's just wet his pants," said Jack. "I know a good werewolf story."

I could feel Hector trembling. I guess he might have been cold, or suffering an allergic reaction to whatever the sleeping bag was made of, but I figured he wasn't the kind of kid to get a kick out of scary stories.

"Maybe we save the storytelling for tomorrow," I suggested.

Jack rolled to his side with a sigh, and a square of

light from his cell phone lit his face. "I've had enough of you two," he said. "I'm going to text my real friends."

I noticed he had a text from his dad. He paused a moment before hitting the view button. All I saw was **Sorry, Junior**, then Jack shuffled farther over and I couldn't see.

I stared at the ceiling of the tent. I couldn't get Dad's silly song out of my head, and started humming.

We're going on a bear hunt. . . .

"Can you shut up?" said Jack grumpily.

Hector rolled onto his front and opened his guidebook, shining a flashlight on the dog-eared pages.

"Speaking of bears," he said. "It's a good idea to be prepared in the event we encounter one in the woods. This is what we should do—"

"Offer you up as a snack?" Jack said.

Hector ignored him and began to read aloud.

"If you encounter a bear, back away slowly. Wave your arms and speak in a calm voice to identify yourself as a human, not a threat or prey."

"Oh, I'd be a threat, Pooper Scooper," Jack said.

"Only if you farted at it, Junior," Hector shot back. "I thought you were texting your *friends*?"

"No signal," said Jack. "Go on, Grizzly Man. What do we do if we meet a bear?"

"Climb a tree if possible," continued Hector. *"If you can't, and the bear attacks, hold your ground until the last possible moment, then fall to the ground and curl into the fetal position."*

"We could throw it the weakest member of the group?" said Jack, nudging me.

"I think we should listen to Hector," I said.

"I still say I could take some stupid bear," Jack said.

Through the open tent flap, I watched the night sky slowly come to life with stars. If you took away the company, the smell of charred fabric and fish oil, the bubbling resentment, it was actually kind of beautiful here.

I woke up a short time later with Jack's smelly foot on my head, a bug crawling up my nose, and Hector poking me urgently.

"Get up!" he said, eyes darting back and forth, the flashlight on under his chin and casting strange shadows across his face. "I heard something."

I pushed Jack's foot away, blew out the bug, and sat up. "Huh?" I rubbed my eyes. Jack bolted straight up next to me.

"No, I won't eat the asparagus, and get that bunny away from me! It's too fluffy!" he shouted, swatting at the air with his eyes still closed. Hector and I stared at him. He slowly woke up and glanced around, blinking.

"What?" he said. "What are you two looking at?"

"Nothing," I said. "Hector heard something outside."

"Oh, quit being a baby, Pooper Scooper," Jack said. He flopped back down.

"That's funny coming from someone who was just trying to avoid a fluffy bunny in his sleep," Hector answered. "Care for some asparagus, perhaps?"

Jack's face reddened and he scowled.

"Hey, I'm sure it was just my dad going to the bathroom," I said. "He's got the bladder of a six-year-old. Goes about three times a night."

Hector flicked off his flashlight. "Maybe," he said. "Just listen."

We stopped talking and waited. Nothing but one of the dads snoring lightly.

"Oh, please," Jack said. "I'm going back to sleep." He thrashed to the side and pulled the sleeping bag back over his head.

Creak.

A twig snapped loudly outside and something crunched across the leaves. Jack bolted upright just as a dark shadow glided across the tent wall.

"Aaaaaah!" he screamed. I glared at him and put my finger to my lips.

"Shhh!" I whispered.

Jack lowered his voice. "What do you think it is?" he said. "The Beast?"

"Most likely a bear," Hector said, bottom lip trembling. "It probably smells our food."

"Or us," I said, sniffing my arm and suddenly wishing I didn't smell like a giant fish stick. I'm pretty sure bears love fish, and I'd be willing to bet a fish-flavored person is a bear delicacy.

"Oh, great," Jack said, scooting as far away from us as possible in the tiny tent. "Now I'm going to be eaten by a bear because of you two and your disgusting bug repellent!" He seemed to have forgotten his claims about taking bears on single-handed in fistfights.

"The best thing we can do is to remain calm and quiet," said Hector.

We clamped our mouths shut, breaths held, as the thing outside our tent continued to crunch across the dry ground.

The shadow began to move away from us. I let out a small sigh of relief, then realized where it was heading—toward our unsuspecting dads sleeping just a few feet away.

"It's going for their tent," Hector said frantically. "What do we do?"

"Nothing!" said Jack. "We stay put."

"It's not your dad!" I said. I sucked in a breath and steeled my resolve. "Only one thing we can do. We have to scare it away. Follow my lead."

"Er . . . nope," said Jack.

I crawled out of my bag. "On the count of three." I slowly unzipped the tent. "One, two, three . . ."

We burst from the tent, hands in the air, ready to face whatever waited on the other side.

BLINDING LIGHT. I RAISED MY ARMS.

Hector cried out.

Jack, somewhere behind me, laughed.

"What the . . ." I began.

I found myself blinking into the beam of a giant flashlight.

"Who's there?" I said.

The flashlight lowered. I squinted and could make out the friendly face of a man wearing a green hat, green button-up shirt, and matching pants with perfect creases ironed down the middle of each leg. Wow. My mom would be seriously impressed.

"Park Ranger Stan Thomas," the man said. He looked like he was nearly eighty years old. He swung the flashlight's beam up the hill. "Saw the car on the side of the road and tracked you folks down here."

My dad poked his head out. "Some trouble, Ranger?"

"No, sir," said the ancient guy. "Just wanted to check that you were all okay."

"Oh yeah," said Dad, rubbing his eyes. "We're fine. Got run off the road by a . . ."

"Fart," Jack said under his breath.

"Herd of deer," I said.

"I'm impressed you found us," said Dad.

The ranger nodded. "Not too hard. I saw the smoke . . . and I followed a trail of these." He pulled a handful of crumpled candy wrappers from his pocket and held them out on his palm, looking at us sternly.

Hector scowled at Jack. Jack sank back on his heels, chewing his bottom lip.

"You should know," Ranger Thomas continued, "littering is a serious offense that we don't take lightly here in the park. Carries a minimum fine of two hundred and fifty dollars."

Hector mumbled something and Jack grunted back. I stepped forward and took the wrappers.

"I'm sorry," I said. "I'm sure it was an accident. They

probably just fell out of my friend's bag. I promise, it won't happen again."

"No, definitely not," Hector said.

Jack shook his head rapidly. "No, sir. It won't."

The ranger looked back and forth between us.

"Okay," he said. "I'll let it go this time. But I expect you to be more careful with your trash in the future. And your fire." His eyes landed on the charred tent. "What happened here?"

"Little accident," said Mr. Lopez.

The ranger nodded. "Been a lot of accidents recently."

"Say what?" said Dad.

"We had to get a chopper out for a broken leg last week. Then there was the lightning storm that nearly fried a family dog. And that's without all these rumblings about Beast sightings."

Jack, Hector, and I looked at one another. *Sightings?*

The ranger looked up toward the mountains, just silhouettes in the dark. We all waited for him to continue.

"Oh, and one other thing." He pointed at our cooler. "You want to make sure to get that off the ground."

"Yes, sir." We nodded.

"Yep," Ranger Thomas continued, "got lots of bear cubs roaming about this time of year. So please make sure to stay on the marked trails. Got it?"

"Yes, sir," we droned.

Jack sucked in a breath. "Sure are a lot of rules," he muttered. "Worse than first grade."

The ranger inspected our faces. "Doesn't mean you can't have fun," he said. "I just want to make sure you behave responsibly. And stay out of danger, of course."

"So, got any suggestions?" Hector asked. "Stuff to do out here?"

"You bet!" Ranger Thomas whipped out a map of the park and unfolded it, pointing to several trails. "There are some great hikes right along here," he said. "You'll see a lot of interesting wildlife, plants, and if you're lucky, maybe even a bald eagle or two!"

"Cool!" Hector said. I could practically hear Jack rolling his eyes.

The ranger continued to talk about various flora and fauna, but my focus had shifted due east—to Bear Falls.

When he was done, I tapped the map. "What about there?" I said. "The falls are supposed to be cool, right?"

The ranger nodded. "Not a good idea on foot at the moment," he said. "The track's quite overgrown, and we've got a damaged bridge roped off. Not stable. If you had a working 4x4, I'd suggest you take the road. It's a bit hairy in places, and about twelve miles. I suppose you could walk it, but it's quite a hike."

"Plus there's the Beast," Hector's dad said.

"All the more reason to stay away from the falls," the ranger replied.

"Yeah, right," said Jack. "The Beast."

The ranger looked at him with ancient eyes and not a shred of humor. The same look the guard at the gate had given us.

"Are you implying that the Beast is real?" asked Hector.

The ranger folded the map and handed it to me. "Can't say for certain," he answered. "Lots of folks have been claiming that they saw something up there. But either way, you don't really want to go the way of Mo Harper now, do you?"

"No, sir," I said, tucking the map in my pocket.

"Okay, I'll leave you fellas be," the ranger said. He pointed at our cooler again. "Just make sure to get that off the ground. And good night to you all." He tipped his hat, and disappeared down the trail following the beam of his flashlight.

Hector, Jack, and I hoisted the cooler into a tree, then climbed back into our tent. Dad was already snoring again, but none of us could sleep. I unfolded the park map and spread it on my lap, using the light from Hector's flashlight to trace the path to Bear Falls. All we had to do was follow the yellow trail up the mountain, then link with the red one to traverse the contours of the slope around to Bear Falls.

"Do you think he's trying to pull one over on us?" Hector said. "That there really is a Beast?"

"I say we find out," Jack said. "We're gonna wrangle that thing and be famous! Well, I will, at least. I don't know about you two. You might get eaten alive."

"But you heard what the ranger said," Hector answered. "It sounded tough to get to. We might not even make it to the falls."

I studied the map. "He was exaggerating. It doesn't look that bad," I said. "If we left at sunrise, we could be there by midday. What do you say?"

"Yes!" Jack said. Hector emitted a small squeak.

"Come on." I nudged Hector and grinned. "It will be fun. We've got to make the most of this trip, right?"

"You might even be able to bag one of the Beast's giant poops," said Jack.

UNTIL I WAS NINE OR SO, I HAD
this recurring dream that I was playing in a band in front
of a huge stadium crowd. I know it sounds cheesy, but
I bet your nine-year-old dreams are too. That night I
had it again. I stood at the front of the stage, gazing out
over a sea of bobbing heads, fingers working the strings
of my guitar like Jimi Hendrix. Over my shoulder, Dad
chilled on bass, Jack punished the drums like a maniac,
and Hector played some sort of keyboard. Mr. Lopez
was on vocals. It sounds awful—right?—but it wasn't.
We were *rocking* the joint. The crowd was jumping. A

banner hanging across the ceiling read: THE WILD BUNCH. HERE FOR ONE NIGHT ONLY!

But as we all leaned into our mics, adding harmonies to Mr. Lopez's melody, I realized what it was we were singing. The lyrics were about going on a bear hunt. Now, that made zero sense because there couldn't be a dorkier song. And upon that realization, things started to go wrong. Hector lost the rhythm completely; I saw him kick over the keyboard. Then Dad's guitar strings snapped and the feedback looped through the mic and speakers, making Jack drop his sticks and put his hands over his ears. I tried to keep going, but Mr. Lopez stopped singing and started talking about the environmental benefits of hybrids as opposed to gas-only cars. The crowd booed. When I looked at the audience, we weren't in a stadium anymore. We were in the hall of my school. And all my teachers and *real* friends were watching. They started to hiss and throw things. I didn't know what it was at first, but then a lump of something brown hit me in the chest.

Poop.

And more of it came hurtling through the air, so much that I had to drop my guitar and take cover. Poop of every shape and size rained down on the band, until it was climbing up my body in a stinking pile.

I couldn't move, weighed down by dung. Higher and higher, until it was around my chest. I saw Hector go under, buried, until just a thin hand rose above the rising tide, fingers reaching desperately. Dad was calling to me, trying to reach across the dung-pile, but he was never getting close. I sank up to my chin, and shut my mouth, holding my breath. I knew it was over the moment the dung touched my lips. My lungs begged for air. I had to breathe.

So I opened my mouth and screamed.

I sat up in the tent panting, and realized at once that it had only been a nightmare.

Some nightmare, I thought. *Analyze that, Freud!*

The other two were still asleep—Hector wearing the same kind of satiny eye-mask that my grandma wears at night, and Jack drooling across his face.

My watch said it was 6:47. Wasn't that the time that Dad dragged me out of bed the day before? My body clock was clearly screwed.

I crept out of the tent. The sun was just beginning to rise, sending streaks of orange and red across the surface of the still lake as though someone had spilled a bucket of paint on it. I cast my eyes in the direction of Bear Falls, following the trail that disappeared into the mist-covered mountains.

I sucked in a breath of cool morning air. Birds chirped in the nearby trees. I closed my eyes and let the rising sun warm my face. Maybe Dad was right—maybe the woods were a place where a person could discover their best self . . . be at one with nature. . . .

Aaagh!

A loud scream rattled the tent behind me. I opened my eyes and jolted as Jack burst through the flap, scratching every square inch of his body. He was followed by Hector, who was clutching his guidebook to his chest and smiling smugly.

"I told you fish oil would keep the bugs away," Hector said with a sniff.

Jack scowled and clawed at his own arms, which were covered in mosquito bites—as were his face, legs, and the back of his neck. I'm pretty sure he even had bites on top of bites. It looked like he'd been stuck with a million pins.

Jack flung his arms around. "It! Itches! So! Much!" he shouted.

Hector opened his book and squinted at the pages. "It says right here that lemon juice will help. And lucky you, we have some lemons in the cooler."

"Ugh!" Jack said, hopping on one foot and scratching his ankle. "I've had it with your stupid remedies."

"Well, it's because of his remedies that we don't look like you right now," I pointed out.

Jack grumbled and stomped off toward the lake, using a stick to scratch his back.

Hector flipped open his guidebook again and tapped me. "I know it's not the safest move, but I'm starving," he said. "Says right here there are several types of edible mushrooms and berries in these woods. Want to help me find some?"

"If it means eating something other than Spam for breakfast, I'm in," I said.

Dad came out of his tent, rubbing his eyes.

"Early start, huh? Great spirit, boys!" he said. "Sleep well?"

"Not really," I said. "We're gonna go forage for food."

"Excellent!" He smiled wide, and I waited for the inevitable speech about the thrill and reward of digging your own wild yams or something. Instead, the corners of Dad's mouth turned down. He pointed at Jack, who was bending over at the edge of the lake, rolling up the legs of his jeans.

"Hey, Jack!" Dad yelled.

Jack didn't turn around. He stuck one toe in the water and pulled it back.

"Ooh," Dad said. "You boys better go warn him to

watch his step. As I recall, the bottom drops off real quick out there."

"Yeah, okay," I said. Hector and I hurried toward the lake.

"Jack!" I shouted. He ignored me and scratched his neck.

"Hey, Jack," Hector said.

"Go away, Pooper Scooper," Jack said. "I'm not talking to you."

"But . . . ," Hector said.

"Lalalala," Jack said, hands over his ears. "Can't hear you."

"Fine, be that way," Hector said, adding under his breath, "but you should know . . ."

Jack took a big step into the lake—and just like that, disappeared under the water. A poof of reddish-blond hair floated to the surface. Jack sprang out seconds later, spitting and scowling, and dragged himself to the shore. Water dripped from every inch of his body and clothes. He shook himself like a giant wet puppy.

"Ugh," he said. "I can't believe this. These are the only pants I brought with me." He glared at Hector again and poked him as he stomped past. "This is all your fault, Pooper Scooper."

"What?" Hector said to his retreating back. "*My* fault?

How is this my fault? I'm the one who tried to keep you from getting bug bites. I'm the one who came down here to warn you. . . ."

I took Hector by the arm. "Just forget about him," I said. "It's not worth the hassle."

Hector sighed. "I just don't get why he always has to be such a jerk," he said.

"Yeah, me neither," I said as I watched Jack sit on a log back at the campsite. Alone. Still dripping and scratching himself. I shrugged. "Maybe it's kinda hard for him, you know, not having his dad here."

"Could be," Hector said. "Still doesn't make it okay to act like a bonehead."

"Eh, you're right," I said. "Now, why don't we go forage? Maybe we can find some extra sour berries for Jack."

"Ha, okay," Hector said.

Luckily we had Hector's book to tell us what was poisonous and what wasn't. We filled our pockets with wild mushrooms, an assortment of nuts—hickory nuts, acorns, and hazelnuts—some juicy berries, and a handful of herbs. I had no idea so many edible things could be found in the forest. It was like we were camping next to a giant, leafy grocery store—but without the annoying carts and screaming kids.

We brought our haul back to camp about an hour

later, and spread it across a foldout table. Dad walked over, stretching. Mr. Lopez followed, eyes bleary, clutching his lower back.

"I feel like I spent the night tied to a plank," he groaned.

"Nothing a few Spam-cakes won't fix, Luiz," Dad said with a clap on his back. Mr. Lopez groaned even louder.

I glanced around the campsite for Jack. His jeans were hanging from a tree branch, drying. A squeezed lemon half sat on the ground below. So maybe he did take Hector's advice after all!

Dad spotted our bounty, grinned, and began chopping up mushrooms and herbs. Thankfully the Spam can had ring-pulls, so I didn't have to work up a sweat opening them. Mr. Lopez dumped the "meat" in the pan with the other ingredients and stirred it together. Dad breathed in deep.

"Mmm, mmm," he said. "Now that's what I call breakfast!"

I looked at the gloppy mess. I'm not sure that's what *I'd* call it, but at least we weren't eating twigs. And it did smell better than it looked, but that wasn't hard, because it looked like someone had barfed in the pan.

"Hey, Jack!" Dad called out as he slid the Spam glop onto five paper plates. "Breakfast is served!"

Something rustled inside our tent. "I'm not hungry," Jack grumbled back.

"Nonsense," Dad said. "You need your energy."

More rustling.

"I *said* I'm not hungry."

Hector and I looked at each other. I didn't mind him being rude to me, but I didn't appreciate him speaking to my dad like that. We were just trying to have a good time.

Anyway, since when was Jack not hungry?

"Don't make me come and get you!" Dad said in a singsong voice.

"Can't I eat in here?" Jack said.

"No room service in the wilderness," Dad said. "This isn't the Holiday Inn!"

There was a huge sigh, more rustling, and Jack finally emerged with a sleeping back clutched around his waist.

"Fine." He lumbered over to an empty log and sat down. As he did, the sleeping bag fell to the ground— revealing a bright white pair of boxer shorts covered in hot pink cartoon hearts. Hector snorted. I had to slap my hand over my mouth to stifle my laughter.

Jack's eyes narrowed. "Shut up," he said, face bright red. "My mom got them for me. For Valentine's Day. Okay? So just keep it to yourself."

Dad glanced in Jack's direction. "Oh, there's nothing

wrong with those," he said. "Should've seen the Batman Underoos I had when I was a kid! Man, those things were awesome." Dad began to hum-sing the Batman theme song.

Jack tapped on his cell phone screen. "Anyone got a charger? I'm running out of battery."

"Sure," said Hector. "I brought one to plug into the nonexistent electricity supply."

Jack turned his back on us as the dads shoveled fork-fuls of Spam into their mouths. I approached mine more tentatively, but it actually wasn't that bad for something that could survive a nuclear Armageddon.

"So anyway," Mr. Lopez said. "Supposed to be lots of rainbow trout in the lake this time of year. Maybe we should spend the day fishing, Bill."

I yawned and took a bite of food. I couldn't imagine anything more boring than sitting around the edge of the lake for eight hours. Sounded even worse than being stuck in a car jammed between Thing 1 and Thing 2 for a day.

"Sounds like a good plan," Dad said. "Too bad the trail to the falls is closed, though."

My ears perked up.

"I know, right," Mr. Lopez said. "We sure used to have fun out there. You remember that time Jack Senior jumped from the top?"

"And we thought he'd disappeared—or drowned," Dad said.

"But he was really hiding underwater using a straw to breathe," Mr. Lopez said with a laugh.

"Yeah, that was an epic prank," Dad said. "Totally had us going. What a wild card he was back then!"

"Wait," Jack said, looking up from his phone. "Are you talking about my dad? When did he do that?"

"Long time ago," Mr. Lopez said. "Must be twenty years now. Before your time."

"Oh," Jack said, and muttered to himself, "Everything fun was before my time."

Dad leaned back, threading his hands behind his head. "Those sure were the days, though, weren't they, Luiz?"

"Sure were." Mr. Lopez nodded in agreement. "Shame the boys can't experience the falls too. The place where legends were made . . ."

"Foes were defeated . . . ," Dad continued.

"And boys became men!" they said together, and bumped fists.

I cast a conspiratorial glance at Hector and Jack. Jack returned a sly grin. Hector smiled nervously. I took a last bite of Spam fritter and got to my feet.

"Hey," I said to Dad, "while you guys are fishing, Hector, Jack, and I are going to do some exploring, okay?"

Mr. Lopez looked at Dad.

"After we've cleared up, sure," he said. "As long as you don't go too far, and you're back before dark."

"You have cell phones, right?" said Mr. Lopez. "Signal might not be great with all the trees, but get to high ground and you'll be fine."

"You got it," I said. Actually, I didn't have a cell phone. Like they did with Jeanie, my folks were making me wait until I was thirteen before they got me one.

"And of course," Dad continued, "like the ranger said, stick to the trails."

"Don't worry," I said, winking at Hector and Jack. "We'll only go as far as we need to. . . ."

All the way to Bear Falls.

WHILE DAD AND MR. LOPEZ DUMPED sand on the campfire, Jack, Hector, and I went to the tent and grabbed our backpacks. Hector read from his trusty guide as we stuffed supplies into our bags.

"First aid kit, rope, compass, water," he rattled off.

"Check." I gathered up gear while Jack watched. I paused and looked at him. "You going to just stand there or are you going to help?"

"Actually," he answered, squirming, "I need to use the latrine."

"Then what are you waiting for? A hall pass?" I said with a wave. "Go."

Jack glanced back and forth, digging his toe into the dirt. "Well, I have to go, you know . . ."

"No, I don't," I answered.

Jack let out a huge sigh. "Ugh. Just tell me, where's the toilet paper?" he said.

My dad piped up from across the campsite. "Sorry, that was on your dad's list too."

"What am I supposed to use, then?" Jack said.

"Your hand?" Hector said.

"A leaf will do," Dad said. "Plenty of those around!"

"A leaf," Jack grumbled as he headed toward the latrine. "What do I look like, a caveman?"

"Now that you mention it . . . ," Hector whispered.

"Ha!" I finished packing my bag and pulled the map from my pocket, tracing the path with my finger. It threaded up through the forest.

"Okay, if we go straight out this way," I said, "that should be the quickest route. . . ."

"Quickest route to what?" Dad materialized out of nowhere and leaned over my shoulder. Seriously, was that guy *always* eavesdropping? I snapped my hand back.

"Just some rock formations that a park ranger told us were cool," I said.

"Yeah, rock formations," Hector said. "You know, big formations of rocks. Places where rocks are formed in a group and make big rocky formations." I elbowed him and made a quick zipping motion across my lips. He clamped his mouth shut.

"A rock formation, eh? Sounds like fun," Dad said. "Maybe we should join you! Hey, Luiz!" he shouted. "Boys are going to visit a rock formation. Want to go along?" Mr. Lopez looked up from where he was stomping out the last embers of our breakfast fire.

"A . . . what did you say?" Mr. Lopez asked.

I jumped in. I had to put a stop to this . . . fast. "No!" I said. "You can't come!"

Dad's face dropped.

"I mean, that would be fun," I said. "And it would be totally awesome to have you along. But then, uh, then . . ."

"Who would catch us dinner?" Hector said, rubbing his belly. "Rainbow trout sounds *delicious*! I've never had real trout right from a lake!"

"Yeah, we don't want to eat Spam for all of our meals," I said. "And you'd better stick around in case Jack Senior makes it."

"Guess you're right," Dad said, the big grin returning to his face. "And real campers don't eat from a can! They catch their own food!" He walked off to join Mr. Lopez.

"You sure about this?" said Hector, when the dads were out of earshot. "Feels kinda like we're being deceitful."

I folded the map. The same thought was gnawing away at the back of my mind. But if we told them the full truth, they'd never let us go. "Look, we'll stay safe," I said. "First sign of any trouble, we'll come right back."

That seemed to satisfy Hector, who shouldered his rucksack with a nod.

"Where's Jack?" he asked.

As if on cue, our companion came hopping out of the woods, face beet red, clutching his butt. He hopped up and down, breathing heavily.

"It *burns*!" he said.

I really didn't want to know, but silly me, I asked anyway. "What burns?"

Tears squeezed from the corners of Jack's eyes as he rubbed his butt. "I used a leaf, just like you said, and now it burns!"

"Eww." I stepped back.

"What sort of leaf?" Hector asked matter-of-factly. "Can you identify it? Did it have five points or three? Was it jagged or rounded?"

"I don't know," Jack grunted. "I didn't sit around counting points! It was green and leafy looking . . . like that." He gestured toward a low bush at the edge of the campsite. Hector's eyes widened behind his glasses.

"That's a stinging nettle," he said. "I can't believe

you didn't know that. Don't you have a garden at home?"

Jack scowled. "Sure we do, but I don't sit around identifying plants for fun."

Hector dug through his backpack and pulled a tube of ointment from the first aid kit. "Here. This will help. But don't even think about asking me to put it on for you."

"As if!" Jack grabbed the tube and waddled wide-legged into the tent. He returned a few minutes later, a relieved look on his face.

"Thanks," he said, and attempted to hand the ointment back to Hector.

"That's okay," Hector said, inspecting the tube covered in Jack's greasy fingerprints. "You can keep it."

I slung my backpack over my shoulders. "All right, let's get out of here!" I leaned in and whispered to Jack and Hector, "You guys ready to find the *Beast*?"

They both nodded, though Hector didn't look entirely comfortable. We turned and waved to Dad and Mr. Lopez, who were gathering up their fishing poles and cooler full of bait.

"See you guys later!" I said.

"Have fun!" Mr. Lopez said.

"Oh, hold up!" Dad said, jogging over, smiling in his enthusi-man way. He caught his breath and held up three soggy Spam sandwiches wrapped in plastic. They looked about as appetizing as an old shoe.

"That's okay, Dad," I said. "Think we'll pass. Hector and I have gotten pretty good at foraging."

"No, take them," he answered. "Never know. You might need sustenance out there." He unzipped my back-pack, dropped the sandwiches inside, and clapped my shoulder. He beamed stupidly at me in that way parents do when you've done something really monumental . . . like not fall off your bike or eat your sister's scented markers.

"I'm so proud of you, Paulie," he said. "Your first time hiking on your own in the woods!" I swear he sniffled a little.

"Paulie," Jack chortled under his breath.

"Yeah, okay. Thanks, Dad," I said, cheeks burning. I hurried out of there before Jack could give me any more grief.

The trail led us around the lake, past other vacant camping areas, then veered up a wide rutted slope that looked like it had been well traveled by 4x4s. The map was pretty easy to follow, and we forked onto a skinny muddy trail after about a mile. We didn't talk much because the trail was steep and narrow for the most part, so we had to walk single file. There were yellow markers every couple of hundred yards that the map said led all the way to the falls, and occasional color-coded signs leading off in other directions.

As the mist cleared, we stopped to rest on a plateau. The lake seemed a long way back already—it looked pristine and sparkling in the early light. I couldn't see the dads, but I thought I could make out some distant singing carried on the breeze. Or maybe it was just an animal dying someplace.

I checked the map again, then scanned the mountain ranges to the south. We had a long way to go—nearly five miles, by my estimate. But once we got up to the red-track level, it would be pretty flat.

We started off again, and I picked up the pace, only to have Hector come to a dead stop right in front of me.

"Hold on," he said, and kneeled on the ground, scooping pieces of dung into a baggie. "Deer!" he announced triumphantly, as if he'd just discovered gold. I waited for the inevitable commentary from Jack, but it didn't come. I glanced back.

No Jack.

"Jack?" I said.

No answer.

"Jack?" I said a little louder, my voice beginning to shake. How long had he been missing?

The thoughts started to tumble through my mind. What if he'd tripped and banged his head? What if he'd had some sort of shock reaction to the stinging nettle? What if the Beast—

Thwack! Something hit the back of my neck and slid down my shirt. I reached up and wiped away a handful of dirt and worms. "Gross!"

A devious laugh came from above my head. I glanced up to see Jack, perched in the branches, holding a slingshot.

"Gotcha!" Jack said.

"Ha. Ha," I said flatly.

Jack leapt from the tree. "You should have seen your face. *Jack, Jack—where are you?*" He cackled again. "And a darn good shot, if I do say so myself."

I snatched the slingshot from his hands.

"It was okay," I said with a smirk. "But I can do better."

I loaded the slingshot with a rock, aimed at a distant tree, and pointed. "Lower branch, left side," I said, releasing the sling. The rock sailed beautifully through the air and hit my target dead on, ricocheting off the branch and falling to the ground with a satisfying thump.

I lifted my hands in the air. "He shoots, he scores!"

"Not bad," Jack said with a nod. "Let's see what you've got, Pooper Scooper."

Hector picked up an acorn and shot it—straight at Jack's foot.

"Hey!" Jack said, jumping back. "What was that for?"

"Oops, my bad," Hector said. His next shot pinged

against a tree trunk. We passed the slingshot around a few more times, until I handed it back to Jack.

"That was cool," I said. "But we'd better start moving again. We've still got, like, five miles to go."

We hadn't made it fifty yards when Hector came to another sudden stop.

"Oh man, Pooper Scooper," Jack said. "Don't you have enough stinky dung for your collection?"

Hector held his finger to his lips. "Shhh," he said in a loud whisper. "That's not it. I heard something."

"Your Mommy calling?" Jack said. *"Hector, Hector! Please come home, my baby, it's naptime!"*

"No," Hector said. "It came from back there. And it sounded like a growl." He pointed into the trees and shivered.

We all stood silently and listened to the sounds of the forest—leaves rustling, animals scampering, birds chirping. But there was nothing there.

Not that we could see at least.

Not yet.

THE PATH FORGED OFF INTO THE forest. There were still markers occasionally, but the trail didn't seem well used, and it was overgrown in places. I guessed it was because of the ranger's warning about the trail being unsuitable. As we hiked deeper into the trees, Jack cracked a branch and swung it like a sword, shouting "All for one, and one for all!" while battling imaginary foes. After a half hour of rattling his sword against the leaves, he ran directly in front of me and spun around, holding the tip to my nose.

"I challenge you, peasant," he said, "to a duel!"

I rolled my eyes and pushed the branch away. "No

time for that," I said, consulting the map again. "We're not even halfway there."

"Sir Hector?" Jack said.

Hector just looked at him.

Jack slashed at the air a few times, groaned, and dropped his sword. "You guys are so lame," he said. "Can't we have a little fun?"

"Sure. We'll have plenty of fun when we get to Bear Falls," I said.

"But it's taking soooooo long," Jack said. He snatched the map from my hands. "Let me have a look at that thing. Maybe I can find a shortcut."

"A shortcut," Hector said. "Not a good idea. You lose the trail out here, you might never find it again."

"Coward," muttered Jack. "Where's your adventurer's spirit?"

"Sorry," I said. "I've already studied the route. The only way to the falls is down this trail and over that bridge." I took the map back—and looked down at it in disgust. There were brown smudges all over it.

"Hey!" I said. "What's this? I can barely read it anymore!"

"Eww," Hector said.

"I don't know," Jack said, shrugging. "Maybe you got it muddy."

"I didn't get it muddy." I sniffed the page. "Besides, that's not mud. That's *chocolate*."

"Hold on, you brought candy and didn't tell us?" Hector said.

"Oh well, hey," Jack answered. "We need to get moving, right? Got to make it to the falls and back by nightfall!" He started down the path. I picked up his tree-branch sword and ran in front of him, holding it to his chest.

"Not so fast, buddy," I said. "Turn it over."

"Yeah!" Hector said, dropping into a Karate Kid crouch. "Don't make me hurt you!"

Jack put his hands in the air. "Hey, no harm, no foul," he said. He dug in his pocket and pulled out three bags of M&Ms, handing one to me, one to Hector, and keeping one for himself. "Was just going to suggest we take a quick snack break!" He forced a wide smile.

"Good idea," I said. We sat on a log. I tossed the map aside and popped a handful of M&Ms in my mouth. Hector emptied his bag into his hands and plucked out all the red ones.

"Here," he said, holding out his palm. "You guys can have these. I'm allergic."

Jack looked at him in disbelief, but took the candy. Hector pulled out his magnifying glass.

"Interesting," he said, leaning over and inspecting a small pellet on the ground. "I'm not quite sure what species this is from."

"Maybe one of your ancestors?" Jack sniggered.

Hector ignored him and reached for his guidebook. But Jack got there first, grabbed it, and started reading.

"Yep," he said, looking between Hector and the dung. "Just as I suspected. That particular specimen appears to come from the Lopezian squirrel, a breed known primarily for its twitchy nature and extremely smelly gas."

Hector reached for the book. "Give me that!"

"Nope!" Jack jumped to his feet and waved the book over his head, just out of Hector's reach. Hector leapt in the air, narrowly missing it with every swipe of his hand.

"Almost!" Jack said, swinging the book away. Hector jumped. "Nope, not quite! But you're getting closer!" Hector was starting to look real angry, and he wasn't giving up.

"Give me my book, you big oaf!" Hector said. He lunged at Jack, knocking him flat on his back. Jack immediately rolled on top of him, pinning his bony legs and arms.

"You really think you can mess with me, Pooper Scooper?" he said. "I don't care if you're a black belt in

Geek Kune Do. I could destroy you with both eyes shut!"

Hector pedaled his hands and feet in the air, trying to squirm out from under Jack's grip. "You might think you have me now," Hector puffed out. "But I am highly trained. . . ."

I reached down and pulled Jack's shirt collar. Hard. He coughed and stood up. Hector popped to his feet and raised his hands.

"Enough!" I grabbed the guidebook and dropped it in my backpack, and positioned myself between Jack and Hector. "We are never going to get anywhere if you two keep fighting!"

"It was all his fault!" Hector said, pointing around me at Jack.

"Nuh-uh," Jack retorted. "I can't help it if he's a giant nerd."

"Am not!"

"Are too!"

"Stop! It!" I shouted. "Truce, okay?"

Jack and Hector's mouths clamped shut and they looked at me. Well, that was more like it. Then I realized they weren't looking at me—they were looking at something behind me.

I spun around to see a gray-and-white raccoon sitting on a log. It stared at us with its masked eyes. And

109

THE WILD BUNCH

in its little black paws it held our map. It was nibbling on the edge.

"Careful!" Hector said. "It could be rabid. Raccoons don't usually come out during the day, you know. . . ."

Jack was reaching for the slingshot.

"Don't you dare," I whispered.

"It's got the map," hissed Jack. "Without that we're toast!"

"Here, little raccoon," I said, hand outstretched. "You don't want to eat that."

The raccoon blinked and took another nibble.

I saw Jack's arm stretching back the rubber bands on the slingshot.

"Don't startle it," I said.

"I'm not going to startle it," said Jack. "I'm going to make it wish it was never born."

And before I could stop him, he fired. A scattering of red M&Ms shot through the air, all missing the raccoon.

It turned, seemed to give a little grin, then scampered off into the woods, our only directions out of this place clenched tightly in its mouth.

"GET HIM!" I YELLED. WE BOLTED

after the raccoon. For something with such short legs, the little critter sure was fast. It zipped between trees, leapt over bushes, and dodged through the under-brush, leading us deeper into the woods—and farther from the trail.

"You just had to get your stupid chocolate finger-prints all over that thing!" I shouted at Jack as we ran. He huffed and puffed behind me.

"I." *Puff.* "Wasn't." *Huff.* "The one." *Puff, puff.* "Who left it on the log!" he said.

The raccoon scurried down a hill, around a tree—and

disappeared. I stopped, catching my breath, and glanced left and right.

"I can't believe this," I said, looking around the forest. No raccoon—or path—anywhere in sight. "It's gone. And we're . . . lost."

"No we're not," said Jack. He ran to the base of a tree, stooped, and picked up the map. "Little critter dropped it."

Thank goodness!

But my hopes were dashed when I got a good look at the shredded paper covered in bite marks, raccoon spit, and remnants of chocolate. A whole section was missing from the middle. Sadly, it included the trail we'd been on.

"Think again," I said.

"Let me have a look," Hector said. He took the map, face dropping. "Oh, never mind." He stuck the map in his pocket.

"No biggie," said Jack. "Let's just go back the way we came."

I turned a full 360. "Which was?"

"That way," said Jack, pointing like it was obvious.

"I'm really not sure it was," said Hector. "That's sort of southwest."

"Fine," Jack said. "Didn't you leave a trail of poop for us to follow?"

"Hector's right," I said. "I have no idea which way leads back. Our best bet is to move forward." I nodded through the trees. "I say we keep up the slope. We'll hit the path again soon. Find a marker. Besides, you have your phones, right? We can call for help if we get really lost."

"What's wrong with calling now?" Hector said.

"And give up on our search for the Beast?" I said. "No way."

"I've been thinking about that," mumbled Hector. "You heard what the ranger said about the bridge being unstable."

"Don't be a wimp," Jack said. "They always err on the side of caution because they don't want to get sued. The bridge will be fine." He started marching straight ahead, his big feet crushing the underbrush and arms pumping. He started to sing in cadence. "I don't know what I've been told! That hairy Beast is getting old!"

I pumped my arms and began marching too. "I don't know what I've been told!" I said. "That big Beast's breath smells just like mold!"

Hector cleared his throat. "I don't know what I've been told!" he sang out. He paused and sneezed. "Uh . . . we're gonna give that Beast a cold!"

We ran out of chants pretty quick. I kept the mountain

peak dead ahead, but after marching for another hour or so, we were no closer to a trail or any sign of civilization. Even the mountain still looked like it was miles away. Not to mention, I couldn't ignore the call of nature anymore.

"Hey, guys," I said, slowing. "Need a quick stop to, uh, relieve myself."

"No need to shout about it," said Jack. "Number one or number two?"

"Two," I said, blushing.

"Watch out for the leaves!" said Hector, as I dodged out of sight behind a tree.

"Watch out for Hector," said Jack. "He'll want a sample."

I tried to block them out as I did my business. There were plenty of leaves all around, but I admit I'm no expert. I fished around in my bag, just in case there were some tissues lurking in the bottom. No luck. I was about to give in and use some foliage, when my eyes fell on Hector's guidebook. Now, don't get me wrong. I respect books, I really do. But in that moment, it just seemed like a better option. Plus, I didn't want to go the way of Jack.

So I yanked loose a couple of pages that were about to fall out anyway. Okay, so a librarian would have been horrified, but Hector didn't really need to know about California reptiles, did he?

I took care of things and went back to where Hector was standing alone, checking out bird droppings on a low branch. Jack was already a hundred feet farther into the woods, running and tagging trees with his hands.

"Hey!" I yelled in the direction of his retreating back. "Hold up!"

Jack stopped and spun around. "Give me a break. If I waited all day for you two, we'd never get anywhere!"

Hector and I jogged to catch up with him. "Seriously," I said. "It's not safe to walk off by yourself. We need to stick together."

"Oh, whatever," Jack answered. "I can take care of myself."

The terrain grew rougher, and we had to climb over gnarled roots and ancient broken branches, and through thick underbrush. Not a sign of a trail or a marker anywhere. I climbed the slick mossy surface of a huge fallen log with a leg up from Hector, then reached down and helped him up. The two of us hoisted Jack to our level, grunting.

"Hey, I'm not that heavy!" said Jack.

When we reached the top we stopped, panting. We were still surrounded by tall trees, the path nowhere in sight. I pulled out my water bottle and gave it a shake.

"Careful not to drink too much," Hector said. "We

don't know how long it will take to get out of these woods."

Jack leapt down to the forest floor. "Not long if you follow me!"

"Seriously, Jack," I said. "Slow down. We should stick together."

He ignored me. I allowed myself two small sips of water, then handed the bottle to Hector. We climbed down too and followed Jack's path of devastation. We could hear his crashing several feet away.

"Jack!" I called. "Wait up."

"No way!" came the reply. "We'll never get there if—*aaaaaaaagh!*" His words became a scream. The next moment Jack came sprinting back toward us, hands over his head and eyes wide. The scream became a word again.

And the word was "BEAR!"

I wailed. Hector farted. In a flash, we dropped our backpacks and raced after Jack. He'd thrown himself up onto a branch, and was scaling the tree like a monkey. I don't think I've ever climbed so fast in my life. I ripped my shirt, and grazed all my knuckles, and stopped in the crook of the trunk about five feet off the ground. We huddled together, leaves shaking, and peered down below.

"It can't get us up here, can it?" Jack said breathlessly, eyes darting around.

"I don't know." My voice was hoarse. "Do bears climb trees?"

"Depends," Hector answered. "Black bears can, but grizzlies can't . . . or is it the other way around? I'm not sure. What did the bear look like?"

Jack breathed heavily. "Big and furry," he said. "And kinda like this . . ." He raised his hands in the air and let out a giant *"Roarrrrrrrr!"*

Hector and I jolted so hard we nearly fell out of the tree.

Jack slapped his hands back down and laughed.

"Your faces!" he said. He screwed up his own face in a terrified grimace, eyes crossed, tongue lolling. "You should've seen yourselves. Man, I wish I'd gotten that on video. It would've blown up on YouTube!"

"Wait a minute," I said. "There isn't a bear?"

Jack snorted again. "No," he said, choking on his own laughter. He gave Hector a small shove. "Never seen you move so fast, Pooper Scooper."

"Not funny, Junior," Hector retorted. "You could have . . . I don't know, given me a heart attack! Or . . . *hives!*" he sputtered, and scratched his arms.

"Oh, come on," Jack said, wiping his eyes. "You have to admit, it was pretty funny."

I felt a mixture of emotions. I was angry. I was

embarrassed. I was glad to be alive. And despite myself, the corners of my mouth twitched into a grin.

"What is the matter with you?" Hector said. "You think it's funny too?"

I nodded. "That fart of yours was pretty epic," I said.

Hector glanced back and forth between me and Jack, and I could tell even he was trying not to smile.

"Oh yeah, well, you haven't seen *anything* yet," he said, slowly lifting his leg.

"Nooooo!" Jack and I yelled.

```
┌ ─ ─ ─ ─ ─ ─ ─ ─ ─ ─ ─ ─ ─ ─ ─ ─ ─ ─ ─ ─ ┐
```
WILDERNESS SURVIVAL TIP #14
REMINDER–ALWAYS REMEMBER TIP #3:
NEVER EAT WHAT YOU CAN'T IDENTIFY.
```
└ ─ ─ ─ ─ ─ ─ ─ ─ ─ ─ ─ ─ ─ ─ ─ ─ ─ ─ ─ ─ ┘
```

AFTER SURVIVING JACK'S FAKE bear and Hector's real fart, we continued, and eventually found what might have once been a path.

"I'm not sure it is a path," said Hector, looking along the overgrown trail. "I want it to be, but it might be our minds playing tricks. Or it could be an animal trail."

"It's better than nothing," said Jack. "I say we follow it and look for a marker."

So that's what we did. It felt good to know we weren't wandering completely aimlessly through the wilderness. Still, it was almost midday, and even the Spam sandwiches were starting to seem appetizing.

"I'm starving," Jack said with a groan. "Why did I have to give all my chocolate to you two?"

"Because you're a kind and generous human being?" Hector said sarcastically.

Jack stopped in front of a bush sprouting plump, juicy-looking black berries. "Didn't you say there was edible stuff out here? How about these? They look pretty good."

"Hold up," said Hector. "Let's check before you poison yourself."

I handed him his guidebook.

"Hmmmm," he said, flipping through the pages. "That's odd. Can't find them in here. They could be edible. Or not."

"Some help you are," Jack said.

Hector shrugged and pushed past Jack. "Well, even if they're not, one won't hurt." He plucked a berry from the bush and held it to his lips.

"Wait!" I said. "Are you sure that's a good idea? Aren't you the guy who's all about being careful?"

"Live a little," Hector said. He shoved the berry into his mouth and chewed. "Actually, they're pretty good." He popped a handful, grinning.

Then his eyes went wide.

"Hector?" said Jack.

120

JAN GANGSEI

Hector's hands flew to his neck and he stared at us in sheer terror. A horrible choking sound came from his throat, and frothy spittle sprayed from his lips. He began gagging, tongue hanging from the side of his mouth. His face turned as purple as the juice on his chin. Then he fell forward, grabbing Jack by the shoulders, and coughed a splatter of half-chewed fruit down Jack's front.

"What do we do?" cried Jack, as Hector spasmed.

"We've got to make him throw up!" I said. "I've watched enough medical shows on TV to know that!"

Hector fell to his knees at Jack's feet, thrashing like a beached fish and spluttering uncontrollably. Then his head lolled back and his legs flopped still. His eyes rolled into his head.

"Oh, God, no!" Jack said. "We need to call for help."

He pulled out his phone and dialed 911. He was about to hit call, when on the ground, Hector began to laugh, his face bursting into a big purple grin. "Gotcha back!" he said.

Jack's eyes narrowed, but a look of grudging appreciation spread slowly across his face. "Not bad, Pooper Scooper. For an amateur, I mean." He clapped Hector's shoulder. Hector toppled sideways.

"Thanks, Junior," Hector said, pulling himself to his feet. "And thanks for trying to save me." He opened his arms like he was getting ready to hug Jack. "That really means a lot, you know."

"Huh, yeah, well, don't get all weird and mushy on me," Jack said, stepping back. "I only tried to save you because I didn't feel like having to carry your dead weight back to camp."

"Sure," said Hector.

"So about those berries?" I said. "I take it they're *not* poisonous?"

"Nah. Just elderberries. Quite delicious, in fact." Hector grabbed another handful and offered them to us. We ate until our mouths were purple and no one was hungry anymore—and no one ever, ever wanted to see another elderberry.

We continued along the possible path, until it petered out into nothing. I tried not to get disheartened. Another steep slope loomed ahead, covered in loose rocks, dirt, and random clumps of grass. Hector stopped at the bottom.

"Let me guess," he said, pointing up. "We're going that way. . . ."

"Can't go under it, can't go through it . . . ," I sang.

"Have to go over it!" Jack bellowed, and began to climb, kicking pebbles and dirt back down at us.

"Watch it!" I said, dodging the spray.

"Sorry," Jack answered, pedaling his feet against the

rocks and kicking more debris loose. I clambered behind him. Hector followed, wheezing the whole way.

Finally, we reached the top and stood on a long ridge that overlooked the forest. The mountain was closer now—straight ahead. Dark clouds were gathering around it. I didn't know if it was because we were out of the trees or because we were higher, but the wind had picked up a little. Certainly there were a few gray clouds scudding across the mountaintops.

I pulled out my binoculars and scanned the terrain. From up here, I could see for miles in every direction. Asking Hector for the map—or what remained of it—I tried to match the valley floor to the contours, but with all the rips and dirt, it was almost impossible. The lake itself was hidden from view behind the shoulder of the hill. We'd come a long way, and though I didn't know exactly where we were, I knew roughly the direction in which we were going.

Hector wrapped his arms around himself and nodded toward the horizon. "Maybe we should head back," he said. "I don't like the looks of those clouds."

As if on cue, the wind picked up, lifting the hairs on the back of my neck. For once, Jack didn't immediately voice an objection. I looked at the mountain, so close yet still just out of reach, and sucked in a deep breath.

"We're almost there," I said. "We can't give up now."

We all stared straight ahead and no one spoke. Finally, Hector broke the silence. "Yeah," he said softly, starting to nod. "Yeah," he said a bit louder. "We can do this."

I pulled out my compass. "Okay," I said. "According to the map, the falls are due east from our campsite. So that means we need to head to the top of the valley." I pointed down the grassy slope ahead of us. "That should link us with the main trail again."

Jack yanked the straps on his backpack and set off wordlessly.

We began to traverse the sloping field, moving through waist-deep grass. I couldn't even see my feet. Every so often I checked the skies, trying to convince myself the weather wasn't getting worse. But there was barely a blue patch remaining now. I just hoped it would hold out until we reached the falls. Sure, all the stuff about Mo Harper and the Beast was probably baloney, but that didn't mean we couldn't have an adventure anyway.

Something rattled in the grass and I froze. "Did you hear that?"

"Hear what?" Hector asked.

Another rattle. This time it seemed to come from behind us.

Hector practically jumped into Jack's arms. Wind rustled through the grass all around our feet.

"Is this another of your tricks?" I asked Jack. The look on his face—pale, terrified—told me it wasn't.

"I think it's a rattlesnake," Hector said.

"Seriously?" Jack said. "What are we supposed to do? Just stand here all day and wait for it to bite us?"

"Rattlesnakes don't bite unprovoked," said Hector. "We just have to be careful we don't get too close."

The rattle sounded again. Very, very close.

"Any other great ideas?" said Jack.

"I know," I said. "We can do rock, paper, scissors— loser has to give the other two a piggyback ride."

"No way!" said Hector.

"Yeah, he'll probably drop me by accident," said Jack.

"And he'd probably drop me *on purpose*," said Hector.

"Well," I said, "I guess all we can do is keep walking. Carefully."

The rattle had fallen silent, which somehow made it even worse. I pressed forward, taking cautious steps, barely breathing the entire time. The others followed, exactly in my footsteps.

I was just beginning to feel good about things, when I felt a sharp pain at my ankle.

I LOOKED DOWN TO FIND A LONG,
slithering thing coiled around my ankle. The pain wasn't actually that bad at first. It was more like someone had tapped me hard. But as I jumped, oh, maybe five feet into the air, I saw the snake wrapped around it, and suddenly it felt like my whole leg was on fire.

"Argh!" I yelled.

Hector and Jack turned and both started laughing.

"Guys! I'm serious! There's a snake around my leg."

"Yeah, right," said Jack.

"Sure," said Hector. "Just don't expect an Oscar, okay?"

I managed to lift my ankle above the grass, and they both backed off.

"Holy cow," said Hector. "That *is* a snake."

I frantically shook my leg, which only seemed to encourage the snake to wrap itself even more tightly around my ankle.

"Get it off me!" I yelled, hopping on one foot and dancing in a circle. "Get it off me!"

"Leave this to me," said Jack. He walked over, raised his foot in the air, and stomped in the direction of my ankle, missing the snake completely and landing his foot with a thud on top of mine. I cried out again.

Hector pulled out his guidebook, and I thought he was going to try beating the snake with it. Instead, breathing heavily, he rapidly skimmed the pages. "Stay still," he said. "Moving around just makes the snake feel threatened."

I took shallow breaths. Were my airways already getting tighter? Was I poisoned? I didn't want to die in a field up a mountain, with just these two for company. My heart pounded. The snake wasn't letting go. Jack slowly circled around me, cracking his knuckles.

"Maybe I could strangle it," he said. "Or set it on fire!"

"Oh, that's a great plan," I hissed through clenched

teeth. "Or maybe you should just chop off my leg. That'll get rid of it!"

"I'm just trying to help," Jack said. "Don't get so worked up."

"Yeah, well, you'd be worked up too if you had rattle-snake fangs deep in your ankle," I said.

"It's not a rattlesnake," said Hector.

"It's not?" I glanced down at the thing wrapped around my leg and quickly looked away again. It was still a . . . *snake*.

"Nope," Hector said. "It's a California king snake. See?" He shoved his guidebook right in front of my nose, then snapped it back and started reading out loud. *"It's native to forests, prefers temperate climates, and only attacks when provoked. . . ."*

"Okay, okay," I said. "But is it poisonous?"

Hector flipped the page, then flipped it back again. "That's weird," he said. "I can't tell. The next couple of pages are missing. Someone's torn them out!"

My cheeks began to burn almost as hot as my ankle. "Um, I . . . ah."

Hector frowned. "What's that supposed to mean?"

"I'm sorry," I said. "It was me."

"You?"

"Well, remember how Jack's dad was supposed to

bring the toilet paper? I couldn't find any leaves to use, so, you know, I had to borrow some pages. . . ." I pointed at my backpack.

"Ugh!" Jack said. "That's foul. You used pages from Hector's book and now you're carrying them around with you?"

"I wasn't going to litter, okay?" I said. I reached my hand around, trying to unzip the back pocket to retrieve them. The snake started rattling. I didn't know what that meant.

"I thought I told you to hold still!" Hector said.

"Well, I'm not getting those . . . things . . . out," Jack said, gesturing toward my bag. "This one's on you, Pooper Scooper."

Hector shook his head, reached over, and unzipped my backpack. With a grimace, he unfolded the sticky pages behind my head and read silently.

"Well?" I said, shaking. "How long do I have?" I tried not to freak out thinking about all the things I hadn't done yet in life: make it to the ninety-sixth level of Mario World, kiss a girl, perfect the double kickflip on my skateboard . . .

Hector jammed the page back into my bag and zipped it shut.

"Nope," he said. "The California king snake is just a harmless constrictor. It's not going to hurt you."

I breathed a small sigh of relief and pointed at my leg with a grimace. "But it's still, you know . . ." I shuddered. "Attached to me!"

"Don't worry!" Jack said. "I got this."

He grabbed a large stick and held it to his lips, pretending to play it like a snake charmer. He danced slowly in my direction, humming and swiveling his shoulders.

Do-da-do-do-do . . .

"Ugh," I said. "How's that supposed to help?"

Jack came to a dead stop in front of me with a huge grin—and in one fell swoop jammed the stick between my leg and the snake.

"Ack!" I screamed as the snake hissed loudly . . .

And released its grip, sinking its pointy fangs into the stick. With a laugh and a quick flick of the wrist, Jack tossed the snake—and what was left of my pride—back into the grassy field.

And then the world seemed to tip upside down.

"I CAN'T BELIEVE YOU FAINTED,"
said Jack. "I'm pretty sure it didn't squeeze you that hard."

I covered the snakebite on my ankle with a small bandage from Hector's first aid kit. Two neat puncture wounds. I was kind of disappointed it wasn't a little worse so I wouldn't look like such a wimp.

"I just don't like snakes, okay?"

"Hisssssss!" Jack said as we began to walk again. I ignored him.

The sun was starting to dip lower in the sky. Three o'clock, according to my watch. We'd taken a heck of a long time to travel not very far, but surely we'd find the red trail soon, and then it was all downhill. We'd make it back before dark, no problem.

We crossed more rugged terrain, scaling a small rock face and making our way through a dense patch of trees. I was starting to feel so fatigued that I was ready to give up, when I slapped a few branches and leaves away from my face and saw it.

"A path!" I pointed. "Look, a path!"

Hector, Jack, and I ran straight ahead, coming to a stop on a gravel trail. A real trail. Not an animal track, not wishful thinking—but a real, honest-to-goodness *trail* with a red marker post. Somehow—and it was sheer luck—we'd found it! A wooden sign read:

BEAR FALLS

ONE MILE

"Yes!" Hector, Jack, and I leapt in the air and high-fived. As we strode down the trail, we took each step with a renewed sense of purpose.

"I can't believe I doubted you guys," said Hector.

"We actually *made* it," I said. "This is so cool!"

"Of course we made it," Jack said. "We're winners!" He banged on his chest and let out a huge Tarzan yell. Hector and I pounded our chests too. Hector's attempt at the call came out sounding a bit like an opera soprano, but even Jack didn't rib him about it.

Sadly, our excitement was short-lived. We rounded a corner and I came to a dead stop. "Oh boy," I said. "We may not want to congratulate ourselves yet. Look."

Jack swung back onto the path and landed with a thump next to me. Hector took his eyes off the trail and stood up straight, squinting. I pointed to where our trail came to a sudden end at a narrow ravine that seemed to run the length of the forest. The old wooden bridge stretching across it had been cordoned off with rope and a large yellow DANGER sign.

"Guess the ranger wasn't kidding," Hector said, swallowing hard.

"So what?" Jack said. "Who needs a bridge? We can jump over!"

Hector's face turned pale. "Jump?" he squeaked. "Across a *ravine*?"

"Why not?" Jack said. "It's only a couple of yards across."

Hector peered over the edge. "It's not the horizontal bit that concerns me."

Jack and I joined him at the edge. It was actually more like ten feet to the other side—not far, but definitely too far to jump. And it was probably no more than fifty feet deep—plenty far enough to kill you if you fell. The base was a narrow creek running between thick vegetation. I inspected the bridge: wood planks secured by ropes, and a handrail running down the right side. The left one was missing, probably washed away in the flood that Ranger Thomas warned us about. I stuck my foot on the first plank and gave it a firm push. The bridge swayed slightly.

"Huh," I said. "It seems sturdy enough. Maybe they just blocked it off as a precaution. You know, since the handrail is gone. If we're careful, I bet we could get across."

"Oh, in that case, I suggest we put our lives in extreme peril and go for it," Hector said, rolling his eyes.

"I'm actually with the bespectacled one on this," said Jack. "I really don't want to die today."

Hector looked shocked.

"But . . . ," Jack continued, "we could play it safe. Rope up, go one at a time."

"What?" Hector said.

"Boo-ya!" Jack shouted.

I was already taking the rope out of my backpack. "All we need to do is tie it around the waist of the person who's crossing. If they slip, the other two can pull him back."

"So who goes first?" asked Hector, chewing his lip.

We both looked at him.

"No, no, no!" he said, shaking his head. "That makes no logical sense. I'm the lightest, so I might get across fine, but then one of you guys brings the bridge down. Maybe you should lead the way, Junior?"

"No, ladies first," Jack said.

"Pig head," Hector retorted.

I put up my hand. "Rock, paper, scissors," I said. "Loser goes first. Ready?" We held our fists in the air. "Rock, paper, scissors—shoot!"

Jack and I both threw paper. Hector made a rock.

"Oh man," he said. "Best of three?"

"Nope," I said, looping the rope around his waist. "Don't worry. We won't let you fall." Hector inhaled deeply and eyeballed Jack, who mumbled "Hopefully" with a wolfish grin.

"Fine," Hector said. He pulled out his guidebook and shoved it in my face. "But the least you can do is tie a proper knot."

I finished hitching the rope around Hector, then fastened the other end to a large tree stump. For good measure, Jack and I grabbed hold of the slack. I gave Hector a nod. "You're good to go."

Hector sucked in another deep breath and ducked under the DANGER sign. He put one foot on the bridge. It creaked.

"You can do it!" I called out. "One step at a time."

Hector put his other foot on the bridge, then slowly advanced, plank by plank. Jack and I kept our hands feeding out the rope, just in case. But Hector reached the end, and with a graceful little leap, catapulted himself onto solid ground.

Jack and I cheered.

"I made it!" he shouted. I could see his legs were trembling.

Hector untied the rope and tossed it back. Jack caught it with one hand.

"I'll go next!" he said. He wrapped the rope around himself and hurried onto the bridge. It groaned in response.

"Whoa!" I said. "Slow down, Jack."

Yeah, that's sort of like trying to convince water to flow uphill. As Jack barreled across, the whole structure sagged, swinging from left to right. "Cowabunga!" he yelled, and leapt off onto the far side, the empty bridge swaying behind him.

"Yes!" He fist-pumped the air. "You're up!"

So we had a dilemma. I could just untie the rope from the stump, fasten it around my waist, and let Jack and Hector take the slack on the other side if something happened. But looking at Hector's spindly arms, I wasn't filled with confidence. The alternative was to leave the rope around the stump and tie the *other* end to myself. If I fell then, the stump would hold me, but I'd be stuck on this side.

"Toss me the rope!" I said. The second option seemed better. If I fell, I'd definitely be alive, even if I was on the wrong side of the ravine.

Jack hurled the rope back across and I looped it under my arms, checking that the knot was good.

"Paul, Paul, Paul!" they began to chant.

I stepped onto the bridge with my right foot. Despite my fears, it did feel sturdy. My shoulders relaxed. Okay, this wasn't going to be so bad. Just a few more steps and we'd be on the home stretch straight to Bear Falls.

Hector and Jack kept cheering.

"We're going on a bear hunt.

Look! A bridge . . ."

I smiled and placed my left foot on the wooden plank. I don't know if it was the sound of splitting wood that I noticed first, or the feeling of sudden yawning weightlessness. I heard Jack and Hector cry out, then my own scream rose above both. My insides turned to liquid terror as the bridge gave way.

I was falling.

I frantically clawed the air, my heart pounding and breath stuttering. The rope snapped tight, banging my body against the side and snatching my breath away. I could hear pieces of the bridge crashing against the rocks below and splashing in the water. Hector and Jack's voices were a muted shout in my ears.

I was spinning, the rope taut above.

"Hold on!" called Jack.

I fastened both hands on the rope, mouth dry as sand. I wasn't going *anywhere*.

"You need to climb!" shouted Hector. Looking up, I saw him leaning over the edge on the far side.

Willing myself not to look down, I reached for a small branch protruding from the wall and used it to hoist myself upward. I lodged my foot between two rocks, hoping for some leverage, but slipped as soon as I stepped. There were no other handholds.

I cracked my knuckles and grabbed the rope, gripping it tightly, and heaved myself up. I don't know if was the adrenaline draining me, or simply that I'd become a weakling, but it was a lot tougher than shimmying up the rope in PE class. Of course, in PE, if you fall all you land on is a pile of cushy mats—not a bunch of jagged rocks and rushing water. I tried not to think about that and instead kept climbing. My arms burned after just a few feet. *I'll never make it. It's too far.* I wanted just to sag back, held by the rope, but I knew if I did I'd never have the strength to try again.

Reach, grip, pull.

Jack and Hector were screaming themselves hoarse. Sweat poured off my head and into a pool on my back. *Reach, grip, pull.*

I thought of my dad, whose crazy idea this whole trip had been. I imagined his face if I didn't make it back. I couldn't do that to him.

Reach, grip, pull.

"You're almost there!" roared Jack.

"Keep going!" shouted Hector.

And finally, fingers stiff like claws on the rope, I cleared the side. I almost hadn't had strength to heave the last foot, but with a lunge, I hooked my leg up over the side and rolled into solid ground, shaking from head to toe. Hector and Jack stared at me from across the ravine, faces pale. I gave a feeble wave.

"You okay, dude?" Jack shouted.

"Yeah," I said, looking up and down the ravine. The problem was, I was back where I started, with no bridge to cross. Fine for me, not so good for my friends.

"You're stuck, though."

Hector dug around in his backpack and pulled out his phone. "I'm sorry, guys," he said. "But I think we can agree that *now* we need to call for help."

I hated to give up . . . not when we were this close. But I didn't see any other choice.

"Okay," I said, defeated.

Hector tapped the screen, and his face dropped.

"What?" I asked.

"No signal." He held the phone in the air, twisting himself in every direction like a human antenna and flicking the screen with his finger. "Still nothing," he said.

"That's because you've got a lame carrier," Jack said. "My phone works everywhere!" He whipped it out and tapped the screen. His cheeks turned red.

"Is that right?" Hector said. "Doesn't look like it's working too well here."

"Well, it *would* work," Jack said. "If the battery hadn't died. What about you, Paul? You got a signal?"

I explained about our family rules, and they both looked at me like I was born in the nineteenth century.

"You know, Jack," said Hector, "maybe the battery wouldn't have died if you didn't spend all your time playing games."

"What are you, my mom?" Jack retorted.

"As if," Hector said. "My children will be geniuses! Not knuckleheads in Valentine's underpants."

Jack shoved Hector. Hector shoved him back.

"Hey! Guys!" I shouted. "No time for that. It's getting late, and we need to figure out a plan!"

Hector fished the half-eaten map out of his pocket

and studied it. "I think the only way is for you to head back to camp. We'll just have to stay on this side."

"What? All night?" said Jack.

Hector shrugged. "Don't worry, I won't eat you unless I get really hungry."

"It's not you I'm worried about," said Jack. "What if . . . you know, the Beast gets us?"

He looked genuinely terrified, and part of me wanted to laugh. But the situation *was* kind of serious. It would probably get pretty cold out here at night, so the sooner I found help the better.

Hector frowned at the map. "Paul, this will get you as far as the junction with the yellow route. From there I guess you just follow it downhill."

He searched the ground, picking up a large rock. He wrapped the map around it and lifted his arm. With a grunt, he tossed the map-covered rock across the ravine. We watched in silence as it sailed through the air— spinning, spinning, spinning . . .

And unraveling halfway across. The rock landed with a thud at my feet.

The map fluttered down into the ravine below.

THE MAP SWIRLED IN THE DISTANT murky water, sinking slowly, until just a curled edge poked up from the surface. Then even that disappeared, taking any chance of finding the path back to camp with it.

"Uh, sorry," Hector said, biting his lip.

"Good going, Einstein," Jack scoffed, and rapped Hector's arm. "Any more brilliant ideas?"

Hector's face reddened. "I suppose you have a better plan, Junior?"

"Sure," Jack said. "We'll just send up a flare."

"Huh?" Hector said.

"Yeah. We can ignite one of your farts, Pooper Scooper." Jack snickered. "That one in the car probably contained enough methane to light up the entire sky."

Hector's face screwed up tight. "I told you already, that WASN'T ME!" He gave Jack a shove, nearly toppling himself in the process.

"Hey, guys!" I yelled. "Forget the map. I think I can find the way."

"*Think?*" said Hector. "What if you take the wrong path? You might end up miles from the lake."

"Yeah, and there are predators," said Jack. "Bears, maybe wolves . . ."

"We don't have much of a choice," I said.

"And don't forget snakes," said Hector. "You might not get so lucky next time."

Something shuffled in the underbrush and a bird flew into the air, squawking. I watched the tall trees sway in the wind, sunlight flickering through the rustling leaves. A small animal scampered across the gnarled forest floor. "I guess you're right," I said. "Well, I'm just gonna have to find a way over to you, then. . . ."

I stared across the deep, winding ravine. Three short yards to the other side. But it might as well have been a mile. I kicked a pebble over the edge, watched it bang down the rocks, and cringed.

"Uh, I'm not so sure, Paul," Hector said. "It doesn't look—"

"No." I shook my head. "There has to be a way. *There's always a way*," I said in my best Dad voice.

I scanned my options. The bridge was completely annihilated. There were no logs to take its place. Nothing on the ground to build a new bridge.

I leaned on a giant tree to my left and looked up. A crooked branch arched right over the ravine.

"I have an idea," I said, pointing up.

"No way!" said Hector. "Even if you could climb that tree—which I'm pretty sure you can't—the branch won't hold you."

"I'm not going to climb it!" I said. "Watch."

I found a rock about the size of my fist and tied the other end of the rope around it.

"What are you doing?" Jack asked.

I took a deep breath and threw the rock over the tree branch. The rope sailed over too, and the rock hung in the air about eight feet above Jack on the other side. He extended his arm.

"Can't . . . quite . . . reach it," he said.

Hector jumped up and swatted the air.

"Wait!" Jack said. He crouched slightly and pointed at his knees. "Stand here, Pooper Scooper. I'll hold you and you can reach out and grab the rope." Hector's eyes grew wide. "Don't worry," Jack said. "I'm not gonna drop you." He flexed his muscles.

Hector looked at Jack, then me, then back at Jack, and finally clambered onto Jack's hands, which were near Jack's knees. Jack lifted him off the ground. Hector reached up for the rock.

"Almost . . . ," he said, tongue poking from the corner of his mouth.

"C'mon, Pooper Scooper," Jack said. "You can do it! Just . . . lean . . . a . . . little . . . more . . . ," he grunted.

Hector extended a shaking hand. His body swayed. His fingers clenched the rock. "Got it!" he exhaled, just as Jack turned his head to the side.

"Oh, no. You didn't!" Jack sputtered. Grimacing, he let Hector fall, then furiously waved the air in front of his nose, gagging and hacking.

"Uh, sorry," Hector said.

"I *knew* it was you in the car!" Jack said between retches.

"Hey, guys!" I yelled, waving. "Over here, remember?"

"Yeah, yeah," Jack said. He grabbed the rock from Hector and braced his weight against it. Hector held on too.

"All right," I said. "Let's just test this thing out. . . ."

I gave a tug. The branch holding the rope bowed a little but didn't break. So I pulled harder, watching for signs of weakness. It seemed sturdy. Well, sturdy enough.

"Think it can hold you?" Hector said.

"I guess we're gonna find out," I said, sucking in a breath. "All right. Hold on tight, guys."

I backed up and got a running start, hands clenched around the rope. Just as I reached the edge of the ravine, I kicked off the ground.

"Ahhhh-ahhh-ahhh!" I yelled. It seemed appropriate. For a second I felt the gap open up beneath me, and I thought I heard a snap above, but then my feet hit the gravely path on the other side. I skidded onto my backside, hands still clutching the rope, knuckles white.

"You did it!" Hector yelled. "You did it!"

"All right, man," Jack said. "Not bad."

I stood, brushed the pebbles from the back of my shorts, and tried to remember how to breathe. My blood was pumping through my veins like liquid fire. *That was all sorts of awesome. . . .*

"It was nothing," I said, holding back a smile.

Hector peeked over the edge of the ravine and shoved his glasses onto the bridge of his nose. "But you could have fallen," he said. "Which probably would have killed you. Or put you in a coma. Or at a minimum, left you paralyzed. And broken most of your bones." He sniffed and pushed his glasses again.

"Uh, yeah," I said. "Thanks for not telling me that *before* I jumped."

Jack laughed. "Yeah, I guess this place isn't exactly boring anymore, is it?"

"Let's get out of here," I said. "We've got to hit a cell signal somewhere."

We followed the crooked trail away from the ravine, edging between tall trees, clumps of thick green ferns, and moss-covered rocks. The mountains towered all around us. An eagle soared gracefully across the sky.

"Did you know," Hector said, "that most birds only have lower eyelids?"

"Huh," Jack grunted.

"And an American toad has a life span of up to fifteen years?"

"Fascinating," I muttered.

"And that squirrels have their sweat glands in their feet?" Hector continued.

"Oh. So that's why yours stink so bad, then?" Jack said, smirking.

"Ha-ha," Hector said.

I laughed. "You have to admit, that was a good one."

"Yeah?" Hector said. "Well, you should also know

then that a squirrel's teeth never stop growing." He bared his fangs at us and snarled. We all cracked up. Hector resumed his random fact generating, regaling us with pointless trivia about skunks, hedgehogs, and three-toed box turtles.

A few hundred feet farther up the path, Jack came to an abrupt halt and plopped onto a large rock, panting. He wiped his forehead.

"What are you doing?" I asked. "This is no time for a break."

"Something in my shoe." He yanked off his right sneaker and shook it vigorously over the grass.

A tiny pebble rolled out.

"You know," he said, "if it weren't for Pooper Scooper here chucking our map in the drink, we'd already be back at the campsite now roasting marshmallows."

"Marshmallows? Don't you mean roasting the tent?" Hector shot back. "Anyway, you think I threw the map in the ravine on purpose?"

"Well, it's not like we could read the stupid thing anyway," I said. "Not with all the chocolate fingerprints and raccoon bites covering it!"

We spent the next several minutes walking in silence, a few feet between us. It was flat now, a track cut into the side of the mountain. I tried to remember the route

I'd come up with when looking at the map in the tent. It shouldn't be far at all now. We'd round the bend and reach our destination. Jack was up front, Hector in the middle, me following up the rear. The path narrowed, leading us through an area of low trees and underbrush. And as we walked, the light dimmed. At first I thought it was getting late, but the time was only just after four. Then I realized it was actually the dark clouds moving in. The wind had picked up again too, plucking at the leaves and branches. The last thing we needed was rain—none of us had even thought to bring a jacket. Not to mention, I was hungry and thirsty.

In fact, the whole expedition was seeming like a bad idea.

Up front, Jack stopped to unscrew his water bottle.

"You should save that," Hector said.

Jack paused with the bottle tipped to his lips. Water spilled out over his mouth, but he didn't even seem to notice. His eyes were so wide I could see the whites around every side.

"Hey, you okay?" I asked. Water was soaking the front of his shirt.

"Yeah, you're wasting it, Junior!" said Hector.

The bottle dropped from Jack's hands. "There's something behind you," he said.

"Oh, please." I sighed.

Hector turned and looked at me, and his eyes did exactly the same buggy thing. He inched backward a few steps. "No, he's serious this time," he whispered.

I grinned. No way was I falling for it again.

"Paul," said Hector, his lips wobbling. "Just. Don't. Move."

Okay, so he *was* a pretty good actor. Both of them were. Jack's knees were actually shaking, and Hector had managed to make all the blood rush from his face. But I was not going to turn.

Then I heard a growl.

I spun so fast I almost fell over.

I tried to curse, but it was really just a squeak.

Less than twenty feet away stood a massive black bear, smacking the ground with a paw so big it made the ground *tremble*. Or maybe that was just me. It shook its oversize head and snarled.

Now, I'd never seen a bear in the flesh before, and on top of the shock, a little part of me was annoyed. All the TV shows had sold me a lie, with their cute depictions of bears. There was nothing cute about this creature. It looked dirty and smelly, and about the size of a small car. Twigs and berries clung to its matted fur, and it seriously needed to see an orthodontist.

The annoyance passed quickly enough as the bear's tiny, bloodshot eyes fixed on me and it raked the earth with six-inch claws. A surge of utter terror made my guts liquefy.

It looked like it had just awakened from a five-month nap.

In a very bad mood.

THE BEAR LOWERED ITS MASSIVE head, fixed its watery gaze on us, and let out a deep, rumbling growl. It looked kind of hungry; at least that's what I read into the drool spilling from its yellow jaws.

I told my legs to walk, and slowly felt the signals trickle down from my brain to my feet. When they moved, they felt heavy and clumsy, and I was worried I might collapse in a heap. By the time I reached Hector's side, the bear still hadn't budged, but it hadn't taken its eyes off me either. I felt like shouting "Why me? What's wrong with those two?"

It shook its head and grunted.

"What do we do?" I asked, throat so dry I could barely get the words out.

"Hold your ground," whispered Jack.

That was easy for him to say. Hector and I were holding our ground between him and the bear.

"The book said to find a tree or something," Hector replied.

I looked around in desperation, but there were no good climbing trees nearby. Just brush and overgrowth. Not to mention, that beast was so close I could practically feel its hot breath on my face.

"Maybe we run," I said.

"No!" Hector grabbed my arm with a clawlike hand. "An adult bear can hit thirty miles per hour. You can't run that fast."

"We don't have to," said Jack. "We just have to run faster than you."

The bear pawed the ground, churning up deep grooves in the dirt, and looked at me like I was a juicy hot dog.

"We've got to do something!" I glanced sideways at Hector, who was now frozen to the spot.

"Forty-two," he sputtered.

"What?" I whispered.

"Teeth," he said, shaking. "The bear. Has. Forty-two. Teeth."

"Gee, thanks," I said. "That helps."

"Jack?" I whispered.

No answer. I risked a look. Jack had vanished. Of all the cowardly . . .

Hector shook his head and sniffled.

"Hector?" I said under my breath. His face turned a funny pink color. "Hector?"

Tears began to squeeze from the corner of his eyes, he blinked several times, and, wait a minute, no, not now, not—

"*AHHHHHHHHH-CHOO!*"

The bear roared, raised itself on its hind legs, dropped on the dusty path, and charged. Dirt and rocks flew up around its massive paws. Hector yelped. I fell to the ground, curled sideways, and covered my head. Hector thumped down next to me. This was it. I was going to die.

Another snort, then silence. Heart pounding, I peeked from beneath my hands.

The bear was a few feet away, shaking its spittle-covered snout.

Hector peered up. "Feint attack!" he whispered.

"Faint what?" I hissed. "I didn't faint!"

"No, *feint* attack! Fake," Hector said. "Trying to scare us."

The bear righted itself and started pawing the ground again. "Well, it's working!" I said.

Something shifted on the path behind us, followed by a *snap* . . . and a *whoosh*.

From the corner of my eye I caught something flying overhead. It struck the bear right on its snout and plopped to the ground. It took me a second to realize it was a balled-up Spam sandwich.

The bear dipped its nose and sniffed.

And—guess what?—someone liked Spam!

With a single munch, it swallowed the sandwich.

I looked back. Jack stood a few yards behind us, holding the slingshot in outstretched arms, one eye closed and mouth twisted in concentration. He pulled the band again. Another sandwich hurtled through the air, landing just past the bear. The hairy beast turned and pounded after it. Jack got a third ready as Hector and I scrambled up and ran toward him.

"Let's go!" said Hector. Jack fired the final sandwich and we ran.

And ran. And ran. Probably faster than I've ever run in my life, and that's counting the time I accidentally spilled hot chicken noodle soup on Rocky MacAlister's lap in the cafeteria (the same Rocky MacAlister who could bench-press first-graders and had been banned from Anger Management after he put the therapist in a triangle choke for suggesting he find his "calm place").

Once we'd run as far as we could, we stopped and doubled over with hands on knees, panting. We stared at each other again, having a conversation that didn't really need words. I'm not sure who started to laugh first, but soon we were all doing it. It was either that or start crying in sheer relief. Hector even tried to give Jack a hug.

"You saved us back there," I said.

"Yeah, no kidding." Hector nodded. "Thank you."

Jack blushed. "No problem," he said with a grin. "Sorry about the sandwiches, though."

"I think we can forgive you," I said.

Hector pulled his cell from his pocket, held it high above his head, and waved it around like a flag. "Still no signal," he said.

"We'd better get a move on, then," Jack said.

We started walking again, Hector keeping the phone in the air like a beacon. We were hot, sweaty, and tired, but at least the worst was behind us. On one side of the path, the slope dropped away into a valley, on the other it loomed above us. We were slowly climbing higher.

We hadn't gone far when Hector stooped to the side

of the path and held a shriveled pellet triumphantly in the air. Jack groaned.

"Squirrel," Hector said, bringing the dung close to his face and wrinkling his nose. He dropped it into his empty M&M bag. You'd really think after filling every single one of his plastic bags he'd give it a rest. But no. Not Hector. Maybe he was actually writing a dissertation on the stuff. Doctor of Dung, Mr. Hector Lopez, for Outstanding Research in the Field of Tiny Animal Excrement.

The air was thick with moisture. It was like walking into the bathroom after one of Jeanie's three-hour-long showers. I could hardly tell anymore if the dampness on my skin was sweat or steam.

"Wow. It sure feels like it's going to—," I started to say, just as a huge crack of thunder crashed across the sky.

In that instant, the heavens split open and rain pelted us from every direction. I'd been in rainstorms plenty of times before, but nothing like this. Anyway, under normal circumstances we'd put up our umbrellas or get inside. Now we were in the open and I could barely see ten feet in front of my eyes. All I heard was the roar of water smashing off the foliage and pounding my skin like falling rocks. Water pooled around our feet, too fast for the hard ground to soak up. As it drenched our shoes, we slipped this way and that, just struggling to stay upright.

"This . . . is . . . ridiculous!" Jack said, losing his balance and grabbing a tree branch for support. "What does your little book say to do now?" he hollered in Hector's direction.

"I think we should take, take . . . *ah-choo* . . . take shelter!"

But there was nowhere to take cover. The wind seemed to blow every which way, churning the trees, lashing branches against our arms. The path was practically a river now, and my feet were as wet as if I were standing in the tub. Small rocks beneath our feet broke loose and washed away with the flowing water. Every square inch of me was sopping wet. It's weird to say, but I actually felt afraid. Of *rain*. "Maybe we should turn around," I yelled over the downpour.

I'm not sure if they heard me. A low rumbling echoed from somewhere high up on the path. It grew louder. And louder.

And closer.

"What's going on?" Jack said. His hair was flattened against his head.

"I don't know," Hector said.

But I did.

The hillside just above us seemed to move, and suddenly the mushy earth beneath our feet shifted.

"Mudslide!" I yelled as the ground gave way completely. I lost my balance and plummeted downward.

WILDERNESS SURVIVAL TIP #19
WHEN STUCK IN THE DARK, YOU
MUST RELY ON YOUR OTHER SENSES—
TOUCH, SOUND, SMELL. . . .

WE SKIDDED UNCONTROLLABLY
down the hillside on our butts, thumping over grassy
patches and—ouch—rocks, screaming the entire way.
Hector did some sort of weird swinging motion with his
arms, like he was trying to swim back uphill. Jack alternated
between laughing and yelping as small twigs and clumps
of earth shot past our heads. For a moment, I managed
to stand, but then tripped over something and started
rolling over and over like a loose barrel. It was like the
whole mountain was collapsing on itself. I half expected to
see Dad and Mr. Lopez sail by on top of the blue cooler,
clutching fishing poles and waving *how-dee-do.*

It could have lasted five seconds, or five minutes, but I slammed to a halt, the wind knocked from my lungs. If that wasn't bad enough, Jack landed on top of me.

I groaned, and looked around. We were in the trees again, lying in what looked like a dried-up riverbed, which was rapidly filling with water from the downpour. Mud dripped from every inch of our bodies. I caught my breath.

"Is anyone hurt?" I asked.

The other two shook their heads, and wiped the smeared dirt from their faces. We all stared at one another in shock for a moment.

"That was even better than the roller coaster at the Great Adventure Amusement Park!" I said, glancing over my shoulder at the hillside. Bits of debris were still slipping down behind us, and rain continued to fall.

"Insane," Jack said. "Totally insane!"

Hector nodded and sneezed. Mud shot from his nose.

I looked back up the hill—or what was left of it.

"There's no way we're climbing back up there," said Hector. He looked like a drowned cat, clothes clinging to his scrawny frame.

"Hey! Look!" said Jack, pointing. "A cave!"

I followed the line of his finger up the riverbed and saw it too—a dark opening in the ground.

"Looks more like a sinkhole to me," said Hector.

"A stinkhole?" Jack said. "Sounds like the perfect place for you to hang out, Pooper Scooper."

"I said '*sink*hole,' dummy," Hector said. "It's a place where the river flows underground. And it could be a good place to take shelter."

We began to squish toward it under the dripping trees. I didn't think it was possible to be so wet. My clothes were heavy, and my limbs ached.

When we reached the hole, we carefully peered over the edge. It wasn't deep—maybe six or seven feet down—and although there was a pool at the bottom, there was dry ground around it.

"What do you think?" I asked Hector. He pushed his glasses up on his nose and reached for his guidebook.

"Hmmm," he said, turning the damp pages. "It would appear . . ."

Jack ran up behind us. "Cowabunga!" he yelled—and jumped in.

"It would appear that we're going in," I said.

"Hey, wimps!" Jack shouted up, voice echoing. "What are you two waiting for? Get down here! This place is so cool!"

Hector and I climbed down the side of the hole. We found Jack at the bottom, standing at the entrance to what looked like a series of underground caves that disappeared into the darkness.

"Whoa," I said, astonished.

"Whoa is right," Hector said. "These must have formed thousands of years ago." He ran his fingers across the smooth rock wall. "You can tell by the level of erosion."

"Looks exactly like the sort of place the Beast would live," I said, a little tingle going up my spine.

"Exactly!" Jack whipped out his flashlight and waved us forward. "Let's do this thing."

He marched straight ahead, singing Dad's campfire song, but with a twist.

"We're going on a Beast hunt, Beast hunt. . . .

I'm not scared!

Look, a cave!

Can't go under it, can't go over it . . .

Have to go in it!"

Jack picked up handfuls of rocks and hurtled them into the darkness. They echoed against the cave walls as we plunged deeper and deeper inside. I could no longer make out anything behind us—except blackness and the faint sound of dripping water. I shivered. It had to be twenty degrees colder in here than it was outside.

We trekked on through the cave. The darkness seemed to close around us, and the hairs on my neck began to stiffen. Then the flashlight faltered for a moment. Jack hit it, and it came back to life.

"Hey, Jack?" I said into the growing darkness. "Tell me you have extra batteries with you. . . ."

"They're new," he said. "I think there must be water in the circuits."

It went out again, and Hector wailed. Jack shook the flashlight and it gave off a few brief flashes of light, then went out completely. I'm not sure I've ever known blackness quite like that.

"Uh-oh," Jack said. "Anyone else have a flashlight?"

"I took mine out," said Hector. "Didn't think we'd be out in the dark. We were supposed to be here and back by midday—isn't that what you said, Paul?"

"Yeah, well, today hasn't turned out quite how any of us expected, has it?"

Jack responded by sniffing the air loudly. "Jeez, Hector! Again?" he said.

"I did not fart," Hector said flatly. "It doesn't even smell like a fart anyway."

He was right. "Smells more like a dog that needs a bath," I said.

"Or my socks after baseball practice," Jack said with a snort. "Yep, that's the smell of victory!"

"Well, I for one don't feel like hanging out here

analyzing cave smells, all right?" I said. "Maybe we can feel our way out."

I took a step back, immediately tripping on something. I grabbed hold of the nearest arm and steadied myself.

"Sorry, Jack," I said.

"Sorry for what?" Jack answered from somewhere across the cave.

"Oh, I mean sorry, Hector," I said, and gave his arm a squeeze. "Thought you were Jack. You're a lot stronger than you look. Your biceps are like rocks."

"I appreciate the compliment, but I have no idea what you're talking about," Hector answered.

Fear began to prickle my skin. "Wait a minute," I said. "I'm not holding your arm, Hector?"

"I think we've already established that fact," he answered.

I gulped. "And I'm not holding *your* arm, Jack?"

"No, weirdo!" he said.

The back of my neck began to sweat, my hand now frozen in a white-knuckled grip on . . . somebody. Or some*thing*.

"Then exactly whose arm *am* I holding?" I said shakily.

A gruff voice spat out one word in response. "MINE."

I dropped my hand in terror as Hector, Jack, and I screamed at the top of our lungs.

A FLASHLIGHT FLICKED ON, ILLU-minating a ghostly face framed by a tangled gray beard and equally messy hair. The man was dressed in a ragged pair of cargo shorts and a T-shirt that had probably been green once upon a time—like, maybe twenty years ago. He glared at us from beneath a set of bushy gray eyebrows.

Jack managed to level the slingshot—hands trembling.

"What are you gonna do, kid?" the man said gruffly. "Shoot me with air?"

Jack kept the slingshot aimed. Hector assumed his karate ninja pose. I just stood there, my heart pounding so hard I thought it might burst through my rib cage.

"Oh, keep your hair on!" the man said. "I'm not gonna hurt you. What in the name of all things good are you doing down here?"

"It's a long story," I said.

"Well, what are *you* doing in here?" Jack asked.

"Yeah, who are you, anyway?" Hector said.

"Name's Moses," he answered, and he began walking, waving us forward. "And I know these caves better than anyone."

"Moses?" I said. "You mean *Mo*?" Hector, Jack, and I shot one another glances as we followed the grizzled old man. "As in *Mo Harper*?"

"The one and only," said the man.

"We read about you on the way here," I answered. "In an old *National Geographic*."

"Yeah," Hector said. "It said that the Beast got you!"

"Then a couple of rangers told us the same thing yesterday," I added.

Mo chuckled. "The schmucks are still saying that, huh?"

"It's not true?" said Jack. "No Beast?" I could hear the disappointment in his voice. Probably envisioning the millions he'd never make.

"What do you think," Mo Harper said, suddenly rounding on me with wild eyes. "Think I'm a ghost?"

I jerked back, not at all sure for a moment.

"People are such idiots," said Mo, with a dismissive wave of his hand. "They'll believe anything you tell 'em."

"But what about the pictures," said Hector, "the ones they found on your camera?"

Mo grinned. "Those were pretty good, weren't they?" he said. "Especially since I had to take them all on film— no digital stuff like you kids have these days."

I was still trying to get my head around what he was saying. It was hard to tell in the dark if he even looked like the guy in the article. That guy had short dark hair, but this weirdo had a gray mane.

"So wait, you just made up the Beast?" Hector said.

"Sure did," Mo said proudly.

"But why?" Jack asked.

"Started off as a prank," Mo answered. "I'd tried to get work as a photographer for years, but no one gave me a chance. So I figured I'd pay them back, make 'em look like fools. Originally I planned to come out of hiding in a month or two, reveal the hoax. But then . . . you know what? I liked it out here. By *myself*." He turned and squinted at us.

"What about your family?" I said. "And friends?"

"The people who matter know how to reach me," Mo answered. "And I don't have much use for the rest of so-called polite society. Animals are better than people most of the time anyway."

"So what do you do out here?" Jack asked.

"Take photographs," Mo said. "Funny, I could never get work before the disappearance, but since then I've had several published in nature magazines. Built a nice little cabin in the woods I've got all to myself."

"Doesn't it get cold here in the winter?" I said.

Mo shrugged his broad shoulders. "Suppose it does," he said. "I wouldn't know. Spend my winters on a house-boat in the Florida Keys. I've won runner-up in the Hemingway look-alike contest three years in a row now!" He stroked his beard proudly. "Now that's enough ques-tions! You boys are wearing me out!"

We continued walking, until I heard the sound of rushing water echoing off the cave walls, growing louder with every step. Soon the cave began to widen and rays of sunlight filtered through an opening up ahead. The water became a roar, and Hector shouted something, but I couldn't hear what he said. It sounded like we were walking straight into a tsunami. Mo turned around and waved us forward with a gap-toothed grin.

Hector, Jack, and I stepped outside, and my jaw dropped.

A huge sheet of water thundered down right in front of us, crashing somewhere far below and sending up a fine mist that dampened my cheeks and clung to my eyelashes. Hector pulled off his glasses and wiped the lenses.

"Welcome to Bear Falls!" said Mo. "Even after all these years, it still gets me every time."

Jack, Hector, and I grinned wildly at one another.

"We made it!" I said.

"Now, step carefully," said Mo. He led us down a narrow trail, around the side of the falls, and onto a small ledge. The rain was still falling, but not as hard, and there were patches of blue sky peeping through above. We were standing about halfway down a sixty-foot waterfall. From here, I had a perfect view of the water as it flowed down the mountainside and barreled over the edge and into a clear blue pool below.

"This is amazing!" I shouted. "Seriously amazing!"

Jack, Hector, and I high-fived. Mo nodded.

"Well," he said in his gruff voice, "you boys made it . . . might as well enjoy it." He pointed at the pool.

I looked around but couldn't see a path to the bottom. "How do we get down there?"

Mo raised his bushy eyebrows. "How d'you think?"

He lifted his arms in the air and threw himself off

the ledge. A second later he hit the water with a huge splash, disappearing under the surface.

"Whoa!" said Jack.

We waited for Mo to surface. And waited.

"You think he's okay?" I asked.

Then Mo Harper broke the surface right at the edge of the pool. "It's more than twenty feet deep," he called up. "I've made the dive more times than I can remember. Nothing like it!"

Jack shrugged off his backpack and nodded. "Now you're talking!" he said.

Hector and I shared a glance, grinned, then did the same.

"Wait!" I said. "We've gotta get a picture of him. No one's going to believe this really happened."

Hector scrabbled in his backpack as Mo pulled himself out onto the bank. With his hair soaking and clinging to his head, he looked half-normal again.

He raised a hand, waving to us, and without another word set off toward the bushes.

"Hey! Wait!" I yelled.

Hector was still fumbling with his phone. He brought it up and snapped just as Mo disappeared.

"Tell me you got him!" said Jack.

Hector squinted at the screen.

"Sort of," he said. He twirled the phone around so Jack and I could see the dark, blurry image of a figure walking into the trees. To be honest, it could have been anything.

"Great!" said Jack. "The National Enquirer will pay millions for that. Not."

"You captured . . . the Beast!" I said.

"Yeah, too bad no one would ever believe it," Hector said with a shrug as he dropped the phone back in his bag. I peered over the ledge as the sun touched the top of the trees beyond.

"Well, guys, it's now or never," I said.

"Who's going first?" Jack said.

"Rock, paper, scissors?" Hector said.

I shook my head and grabbed each of them by the hand. "Nope," I said. "We go together. All for one and one for all! Three . . . two . . . one . . . ," I counted.

"Cowabunga!" Jack yelled—and we leapt from the side, plummeting into the pool below with a fantastic splash.

```
┌────────────────────────────────────────────┐
│                                              │
│   WILDERNESS SURVIVAL TIP #21                │
│   THE PATH BACK HOME IS NOT                  │
│   ALWAYS THE WAY YOU CAME.                   │
│                                              │
└────────────────────────────────────────────┘
```

THE WATER WAS COOL AND CLEAR
and smelled like early summer rain. Jack swam in circles, pretending to be a shark. Hector did some sort of modified doggy paddle back and forth across the pool. I floated on my back, staring up at the sky and listening to the rhythmic pound of water rushing over the falls. This trip hadn't turned out to be a disaster after all.

In fact, it was shaping up to be pretty awesome.

Jack circled underwater, hand above the surface like a dorsal fin, and yanked my foot. I splashed him when he popped up for air. Hector snorted out a laugh and sneezed. We horsed around like that for a good half hour.

Finally, I swam to the edge and pulled myself up on the rocks. The sun was setting, casting orange and purple streaks across the sky.

"Guys," I said, "it's gonna be dark soon. We'd better get back to camp."

We climbed up to the ledge and grabbed our backpacks, then followed the path back to the main road. We were all dripping wet, but it was better than being caked in mud. A sign pointed away from the falls:

LAKE CAMPSITE 10 MILES

"Ten miles?" Jack said. "I don't think I can walk another ten *feet*!"

"There's no way we can make it that distance before it gets dark," I said. Despite all the fun we'd had, I felt pretty guilty. We'd promised we'd get back by nightfall. Dad would be really worried.

"Hey!" said Hector, holding up his phone. "I've got a signal!"

"What are you going to say?" Jack asked.

"I dunno," Hector said with a shrug. "The truth?"

I thought about it. The thieving raccoon, the snakebite, the encounter with the bear, the ravine escape, the mudslide, and meeting a man who disappeared three decades ago. It would sound 100 percent crazy.

"Maybe just say we got lost?" I said.

But before Hector could hit call, a green Jeep with an open top rumbled around the corner and stopped right before us, spitting up pebbles. I dunno, but after being out in the wilderness so long, the sight of something so artificial was as strange as if an alien had just landed in front of us. Hector dropped the phone in his pocket. I waved when I recognized the old guy climbing out of the front seat.

The ranger's face was stern. "How the heck did you guys get up here?" he said. "Thought I told you it wasn't safe."

"Uh-huh," I stammered, shoving my hands in my pocket. "We just walked the road, like you said."

The ranger looked hard at me. "Is that right? 'Cause a little bird told me you came through the caves."

"Wait! You know Mo Harper?"

"Sure I do," said the ranger. "I've worked here going on forty years. Now, you boys need a lift back to camp or what?"

"Yes, please!" said Jack.

We grabbed the roll bar and hopped inside. There was a bunch of radio equipment on the front seat, so I found myself wedged in the back between Jack and Hector. As usual. Ranger Thomas turned the Jeep around and we rumbled down the road.

"Hey," I said as he drove. "What about the Beast? If you know Mo, you know that story is nonsense."

The ranger's eyes glanced in the rearview mirror. He grinned. "Mo and I play cards sometimes. He values his privacy. Doesn't do me any harm to keep his secret."

He sped up, rumbling the Jeep downhill and around sharp bends. The warm evening wind whipped against our faces. It smelled like damp grass and smoky camp-fires. I sucked in a deep breath. Yeah, this place really wasn't half bad.

Ranger Thomas came to a sudden stop at the side of the road. Hector, Jack, and I grabbed the roll bar to keep from lurching forward. The ranger threw the Jeep into park and turned around.

"Here you go, boys. Your campsite is a half mile straight down that path," he said, pointing. "I trust you can find your way."

"Thank you for the ride," I said as we climbed from the car. I was stiff all over and covered in bruises, but other than that, I felt pretty good.

"You're welcome," he answered. "Now before you go, I need you to make me a promise not to tell anyone what you saw up there."

"Are you kidding?" said Jack. "We just solved the mystery of Bear Falls!"

The ranger looked at him sternly. "I need you to promise."

Jack looked like he was about to complain again, but then stopped. He shot a glance at Hector and me. I shrugged. "What good will it do anyone?" I said. "All we've got is Hector's picture anyway. No one will believe it."

Jack sighed. "All right, then."

"We promise," said Hector.

The ranger smiled. "You're good kids. Enjoy the rest of your weekend. And please, stay on the marked paths from now on!"

With that, he threw the Jeep into drive and peeled away.

Hector, Jack, and I began the short walk back toward camp.

"So are we going to tell the grown-ups we even went to the falls?" Hector asked, bony shoulders slumping. "My parents will be angry."

"It's so annoying, but I don't think we should say anything," I said.

"Mine wouldn't care one way or the other," muttered Jack.

I looked at him. He seemed kind of sad, but I didn't know what to say.

"So it's our secret," I said. "Let's shake on it." I spat in my palm and held out my hand. Hector wrinkled his nose and spat in his. Jack did the same.

"All for one and one for all," I said as we shook. Jack pulled his hand away, and with a smirk, wiped it on Hector's back.

"Eww!" Hector said with a shudder.

"You're welcome," Jack answered. "That's for the car fart!"

"How many times do I have to tell . . . ," Hector started, then huffed out a sigh. "Oh, okay. It *was* me. And it was a pretty good one, wasn't it?"

We cracked up, and kept walking until we reached a small clearing. I could see the points of our tents and could hear the crackle of the campfire. The smell of roasting fish filled the air. My mouth began to water; I was officially starving.

"Hey, Dad!" I said with a wave as we rounded the corner. He was sitting on a log opposite Mr. Lopez. There were two cars parked nearby—one a new 4x4 with the same rental company logo, and the other a flashy sports car. A guy wearing a suit was standing to one side, typing something on his phone. I didn't need to be introduced to know it was Jack Senior. Father and son carried themselves exactly the same way.

"There you are," Mr. Lopez said, standing up quickly.

"I was just starting to get worried you'd been eaten by wolves, but Paul's dad said you'd be back on time."

I glanced at my friends and grinned. Wolves were about the only creatures we *hadn't* met.

"Nothing to worry about," I said. "Just having a good time exploring."

Mr. Gracie glanced up from his phone and inspected his son with a scowl. "You're all wet and muddy, Jack," he said. "*And* you've ruined another pair of jeans? That's the second pair this month!"

"Just got caught in the rain, sir," Jack said, face red and shoulders slumping. Suddenly he looked two years younger. "Sorry."

Mr. Gracie grumbled something under his breath and went back to typing. Jack, Hector, and I grabbed spots side by side on a log and warmed our hands in front of the fire. A huge salmon sizzled in the skillet above it. Mr. Lopez waggled his eyebrows and pointed.

"So, while you boys were out discovering nature, we caught ourselves the *real* Beast of Bear Falls," he said.

I had to bite my lip to keep from laughing. They had no idea. . . .

"Yep," Dad chimed in. "Took us *all afternoon* to land that bad boy. He wasn't going down without a fight, that's for sure!"

Mr. Lopez laid the skillet on a rock and divided up the salmon onto our plates, telling us that the rental place had come by with a new vehicle just after we left. I took a bite and exhaled happily, eyes closed. No question; it was possibly the best fish I'd ever tasted.

"So," Dad said. "Tell us about your exploring, boys. See anything interesting?"

"A little of this and a little of that," I said. "You know, just checking out the woods."

"Yeah, we saw this crazy raccoon . . . ," Jack said.

His father glanced at him. "Don't talk with your mouth full," he scolded. "It's rude."

"Yes, sir." Jack sank back.

I scraped the last few morsels of salmon from my plate, then got up to throw the bones in the trash. As I stuffed them in the bag, I noticed a very suspicious-looking white paper wrapper hiding beneath some empty Spam cans. I turned my head sideways and read the label:

Fresh salmon, $12/pound

It looked like Hector, Jack, and I weren't the only ones who might have been fudging the truth today. . . .

I CRAWLED INTO MY SLEEPING

bag that night to the chirp of insects and the rustling of leaves—my muscles tired, eyes heavy, and stomach full. Jack's dad had bought a brand-new replacement tent on the way up, but Jack chose to crash with us instead. Even with both of them beside me, it was the best sleep of my life.

The next morning, as we loaded up, Ranger Thomas came to see us off. He touched the side of his nose and pointed to me, Jack, and Hector. I looked back at the mountain in the distance, shrouded in mist, and wondered if Mo Harper would ever reveal his secret. But then

I decided it didn't really matter. He was happy, he wasn't harming anyone, and that was all that counted.

Not to mention, he pretty much had the coolest bathtub and shower in the entire world. Even if he didn't use it often enough.

Jack stuffed his bag into Mr. Gracie's car. When we were done loading the car, Dad leaned on the open passenger side door of the rental and smiled wide.

"So, what did you think, boys?" he said. "Have fun?"

We shrugged and looked at one another. "It wasn't bad," I said with a smirk. "Saw a few interesting things."

"Yeah." Dad leaned in conspiratorially. "About that . . . you know, the little accident with the fire, and the, ahem, deer, and all that . . . we should probably keep that stuff to ourselves. If we want Mom to let us go anywhere again, that is." He stood up straight, voice booming. "And you boys want to go on another trip, right?"

Hector, Jack, and I looked at each other.

"Sure," Hector said. "As long as I don't have to listen to Jack talk in his sleep again."

"And I'm not going anywhere that he can scoop up poop." Jack waggled a finger at Hector.

"I'll go *anywhere* I don't have to listen to these two argue," I said. "Maybe a very loud concert."

"I'd much rather go to a nice quiet museum," Hector said.

"What?" Jack said. "Hunting. I vote for big game hunting!"

"I'll take that as a yes, then," Dad said. He stretched out his hand. "To the Wild Bunch, right?"

At the beginning of the weekend I would have cringed, but after a pause, I placed my hand on top of Dad's. Hector and Jack laid theirs on too.

"To the Wild Bunch!" we said together.

Mr. Gracie peered into Mr. Lopez's trunk, saw us, and screwed up his face. "Mind if I grab a water before we ship out?" he said.

"No problem, Jack," Mr. Lopez said. "Help yourself."

Mr. Gracie flipped open the blue cooler. "Oh, hey!" he said. "M&Ms. My favorite. Don't mind if I do!"

We watched him tip the packet straight into his mouth. I guess we *could* have stopped him, technically. But Jack, his own son, said nothing. And even Hector, who was losing his hard-won poop collection, didn't speak up.